The
Innkeeper's
Daughter

Also by Barbara Cohen

Benny

The Binding of Isaac

Bitter Herbs and Honey

The Carp in the Bathtub

R My Name Is Rosie

Thank you, Jackie Robinson

Where's Florrie?

The Innkeeper's Daughter
Barbara Cohen

Lothrop, Lee & Shepard Books
New York

J
C

1 2 3 4 5 6 7 8 9 10

Library of Congress Cataloging in Publication Data
Cohen, Barbara.
   The innkeeper's daughter.
   SUMMARY: Helping her widowed mother run a small inn provides 16-year-old Rachel with many opportunities to adjust to growing up.
   [1. Hotels, motels, etc.—Fiction]   I. Title.
PZ7.C6595In   [Fic]   79-2421
ISBN 0-688-41906-2   ISBN 0-688-51906-7 lib. bdg.

For Sara
who is also an innkeeper's daughter

The Innkeeper's Daughter

I

Mr. Jensen was sleeping in my room again. I despised giving up my bed to him and spending the night in Rosie's room. I never got used to it, even though it happened at least once a week. All right, so maybe it wasn't once a week. Maybe it was twice a month. But it seemed like every night.

"Why me?" I asked my mother. "Why is it always me? Why can't Mr. Jensen sleep in Dan's or Rosie's room once in a while?"

"Because Rosie has twin beds. If I gave her room to Mr. Jensen, she'd have to share your double bed with you," my mother explained, with irrefutable logic. "Would you like that?"

"You know perfectly well I wouldn't like it," I retorted. "So what about Dan's room?"

Her logic wasn't quite so irrefutable this time. "Dan's room is so small," she replied, "and it's pasted all over with pictures of baseball players and jazz musicians. I don't think Mr. Jensen would be comfortable in there."

"Well, I think you're doing him a big enough favor as it is," I said, "always giving him a room, no matter what time he shows up. He really doesn't have any right to care if it's comfortable or not."

"Oh, he never says anything," my mother assured me. "He's very appreciative. He's grateful to you, too. He's a very good customer, Rachel, a very good customer—as well as a good friend."

I wasn't satisfied, but there wasn't anything I could do about it. My mother ran a small hotel on the outskirts of Waterbridge, New Jersey, and I knew I ought to be thankful that Mr. Jensen was the only customer to whom she had absolutely guaranteed a room. She had told me when I had begged her for my own room that I could have it, but that I should expect to have to give it up once in a while, if she needed it for a really good customer. And then she had bought me a beautiful four-poster bed at an auction, and a marvelous old Victorian desk she'd noticed rotting away on her hairdresser's storm porch. She must have gotten me just about the first room air-conditioner to come on the market, because I suffered miserably from hay fever. The air-conditioner not only cooled but also filtered the air. So, while everyone else in the Waterbridge Inn sweated through wakeful, hot July nights, I slept in serene, air-conditioned comfort. But, of course, there was a catch. If Mr. Jensen came when the Inn was full, I had to give him my room. I never got used to it. Thomas Wolfe would have understood. Last spring when I had read *Look Homeward Angel,* I had discovered there were other people besides me who reluctantly gave up their beds to paying guests.

"Listen, Mother," I said, "I don't like living at an inn. I just don't like it."

"Someday," Mother said, "when I can afford it, I'll buy a house. But now I can't spend any time away from this place, and I want you here, where I can keep an eye on you."

Not much of an eye—which was, of course, at times an advantage. She was so busy that usually we didn't even eat our meals with her. Dan and Rosie couldn't remember any other kind of life. However, I could. I could remember before Dad died, before he bought the Inn, before we moved to Waterbridge. I could remember when we were ordinary people.

"When's he coming?" I asked. "When will Mr. Jensen get here?"

"Oh, not 'til ten. He just called. He has to work late; that's why he can't go home tonight." Mr. Jensen lived in Morristown, about twenty miles away along a narrow, dark, twisting road, which is why he spent so many nights at the Inn. Or at least that was one reason. There were others, and I knew it.

I had lots more to say on the subject of Mr. Jensen, but my mother had turned her attention to the green loose-leaf notebook in which she kept all the information about every banquet and reception held at the Waterbridge Inn. That notebook was my mother's bible and, once she had her head in it, I certainly wasn't able to distract her.

Anyway, it was time for dinner. I wandered out of the office and into the Holiday Room. "The Holiday Room" was the name with which Mother had enobled the big room used for banquets. The smaller, public dining room she called "The Colonial Room."

Dan, Rosie, and I ate dinner early, before the dining room got busy or any party booked for the evening got underway. Mother rarely ate with us because she liked to relax over her meal after the rush. We sat at our table by the kitchen door sometime around five-thirty and listened to Dan's portable radio while we ate. Every afternoon we listened to "Jack Armstrong, All-American Boy," "Terry and the Pirates," "Captain Midnight," and "Tom Mix." Even I listened, though I was sixteen and wouldn't have let on to a soul that I still cared about what happened to Tom Mix.

"Take a tip from Tom, Go and tell your Mom, Hot Ralston can't be beat." Just as the radio began playing that tinny little tune, Mother came in and sat down with us. Sometimes she did that when she had a few minutes to spare. Min, the head waitress, brought her a cup of coffee and she drank it while we ate our roast beef and baked potatoes.

"Today we got to the part in our health book about the evils of alcohol," Dan said, turning to me. "Did they hand you that lecture when you were in eighth grade?"

I almost choked on a string bean, but I managed to mumble, "Sure." Did they hand me that lecture in eighth grade? I could still see the black letters on the white page of the health book screaming at me that after even one drink you couldn't walk straight and your liver would commence an irreversible decline. I had been so upset that I had never been able to even talk about it. That same year Mother and I had gone shopping in New York City one hot day and, when we got to Stouffer's for lunch, Mother drank two frozen daiquiries. I watched her down the first one without any visible reaction, but when she ordered the second one I burst into tears. To this day, she didn't know why I had cried. It seemed incredible to me that Dan could talk about that alcohol chapter as easily as if it were the one on the digestive system.

"Dumb," Dan said. "That chapter is so dumb. Everyone knows Mr. Almarle drinks like a fish, and there he is telling us how one sip leads to skid row. When they exaggerate so much, you don't believe any of it."

"Well, alcohol isn't *good* for you," I offered hesitantly. "Everyone knows that. I think it's too bad Mother has to make her living selling it."

"Make *your* living," Mother interrupted drily. "Do you have some better idea as to what I might do?"

"You could teach, like you did before you were married," I suggested.

"I hated teaching," Mother replied. "I wasn't cut out for it. On a teacher's salary do you think you'd be sitting around eating roast beef or steak for dinner every night? The Inn may not show a profit, but at least we live well." That was an old story. She always said, "You don't get rich in the restaurant business, but you don't starve either."

"Boy, are you a jerk," Dan said. "How many drunks have you seen around here lately? Tex won't even serve someone he thinks has had too much." Tex was the bartender. "Just because you take one drink doesn't mean you're going to be an alcoholic."

"On the other hand," I countered, "you can't get to be an alcoholic unless you *do* take that first drink."

"If you're so worried about it, don't you ever take one," Mother said. "You can even skip the wine when we go to Aunt Faye's for Passover."

"Yeah," Dan agreed, "if alcohol is so bad, why do Jews and Catholics drink it all the time as part of their religion? It's only some Baptists and dumb people like that who are against it."

"What do they know?" Rosie interjected cheerfully, with a wave of her hand.

"That's a prejudiced remark," I said. "I don't like it. You'd be furious if you heard someone calling Jews dumb!"

"You're a hundred percent right, Rachel," Mother said. "Which reminds me—you got a letter today. I forgot to give it to you when you were in the office earlier. It looks like an invitation."

I didn't see the connection, but I was glad she had remembered it. She left the table and came back a few minutes later with a white envelope. She, Rosie, and Dan sat staring at me while I looked it over. It was from Sally Stewart and, when I saw that, I knew why a conversation about prejudice had reminded Mother to give it to me. The Stewarts were high society in Waterbridge. People like them didn't have much to do with people like us, outside of business.

"Open it already, will you?" Rosie said. "Don't just sit there staring at it like a codfish."

"What are you so curious about?" I asked. "It's my letter. I don't have to tell you what it says." But I opened it.

"Well," Mother asked, "what is it?"

"Just what you thought," I replied. "An invitation. Sally's invited me to a party."

"How nice of her to remember you after all these years," Mother said. "Her mother is really so much nicer than most of those other Civic League ladies."

I wasn't surprised that Sally had remembered me. I certainly hadn't forgotten her. She and I had been good friends in grammar school but, after we were graduated from eighth grade, her parents had sent her to a famous, old Quaker boarding school outside of Philadelphia. I missed her. She was the only friend I'd ever had who liked to read as much as I did. We had spent hours in elaborate make-believe inspired by our favorite fairy stories. Once we'd even turned a book we liked into a play, which we put on in Sally's double parlor, charging the kids in her neighborhood a nickle each to watch it. It was a good play, based on *Thee Hannah* by Marguerite de Angeli, and we wore marvelous, authentic Civil War costumes that we'd found in Sally's attic. We were in sixth grade then. We were never so close again and hadn't seen each other at all since Sally'd gone off to Penn Manor.

"When is the party?" Mother asked.

"The Saturday after Thanksgiving."

"I'll get you a new dress," she said.

I hadn't even had to ask. This time my mother knew how important the occasion was. I wondered which other kids from town Sally had invited. Maybe one of them was Billy Colbert. I sort of loved Billy Colbert, only he didn't know it. After all, a person had to love somebody besides Peter Lawford, though what I'd do if Billy Colbert actually touched me I wasn't at all sure. Still, I wanted him to be aware of me as something other than the resident brain. Maybe, if we were both at the same party, something would happen that would make him notice me. Like Rosie, I was kind of fat. The only skinny one among us three was Dan, who didn't eat anything. Right now, the baked potatoes and the string beans and half the roast beef sat congealing on his plate.

I was also kind of messy. I knew it, and told myself I was too busy with other things—like the school news-paper and dramatics and books and helping around the Inn—to bother with how I looked. But even I knew what I told myself wasn't the truth. I did care about how I looked; I just didn't think there was anything I could do that would make any difference.

But, with a new dress and some help from my mother, who could tell? I might get Billy Colbert to look at me in a whole new way if he saw me in a whole new place. The more I thought about it, the surer I was that he would be there. We had all been in the same class from the time I'd moved to town right through the eighth grade. If Sally had invited me, she'd certainly have invited Billy Colbert.

Rosie poked at me with her finger. "Hey, Rachel, answer me."

I looked at her, startled. "Did you say something? I didn't hear you."

"She's dreaming," Dan said. "She's dreaming of Billy Colbert." He noticed a lot more than he let on.

"Who's Billy Colbert?" Mother asked.

"Shut up," I said to Dan, automatically. I turned back to Rosie. "What do you want?"

"What kind of dress are you going to get?"

"We'll have to go down to La Mode," Mother said, "and see what they have."

"Nothing little girl," I insisted. "Not like that horrible purple disaster I had to wear last spring to Dan's bar mitzvah."

"It has to meet two criteria," Mother said. "It has to fit you and it has to be something I can afford."

"And we both have to like it," I reminded her. That was our agreement, entered into after the nightmare in purple. If either of us didn't like it, it didn't get bought.

"Yes," she agreed, "we both have to like it. You can wear it to the Inn's Christmas party, too, and on New Year's Eve."

"New Year's Eve? You mean you're going to let me work this year?" I was really pleased. The money was good New Year's Eve. Besides, it was something to do.

"You can run the cloakroom," Mother said. "You're old enough."

"I've been old enough for centuries," I told her.

"You can work, too," she said to Dan, "if you want to."

"I don't want to," Dan said.

"I didn't think so," Mother said.

"I want to," Rosie said.

"You *are* too young," Mother said.

"What am I supposed to do?" Rosie complained, her eyes filling up with easy tears. "Sit upstairs all by myself New Year's Eve?"

"You'll be with Dan," Mother said.

"Dan!" Rosie snorted. "He'll be fast asleep by ten-thirty. The only thing he stays up for is a ball game, and even I know there are no ball games New Year's Eve."

"More's the pity," I said, "so far as Dan's concerned."

Dan nodded a vigorous agreement.

"Maybe you can invite a friend to sleep over," I suggested.

Rosie snorted again. "Right now the only friend I have is Bart, and you can't invite a boy to sleep over."

"No, I guess not," I admitted.

"We'll work something out," Mother said. "Don't worry about it."

Mother always said, "We'll work something out. Don't worry about it." It was her creed. Our father had died of a heart attack, leaving her, at the age of thirty-two, with three children and a run-down Inn he had bought the year before. Money was so short then, she'd had to borrow from Aunt Faye to bury him. Now, just seven years later, besides plenty to eat, there were music lessons, occasional trips to ball games or the theatre, and new dresses for Rosie and me when we needed them. We weren't starving. We weren't going barefoot. But we three worried about other kinds of things—things she was just too busy to notice, or didn't consider important enough to concern herself with.

Since Mr. Jensen wasn't coming until ten o'clock, I went upstairs to my room and did my homework in comfort. I was writing a research paper on the relationship between the Elizabethan pastoral romance and Shakespeare's *As You Like It.* In junior English you had to write a research paper in order to learn techniques of notetaking, footnoting, and all those picayune little things. You weren't supposed to care all that much about the actual material you were researching. But I loved the things I was reading for this paper. They were pulling me into them; and my desk, with its neat piles of index cards and musty books I'd borrowed from the Rutgers library, had become a remote and wonderful world to me.

I worked on the paper for about an hour, did my chemistry assignment, which I didn't care for nearly as much, put fresh linen on my bed for Mr. Jensen, changed into my nightclothes, took the book I was reading and all the things I'd need for school in the morning, and crossed the hall to Rosie's room.

The room was an incredible mess. I swept the piles of clothes and dolls on the extra bed right off onto the floor. There wasn't any point in trying to arrange them neatly some place, since there wasn't a surface anywhere that was not equally littered. About seventeen stuffed animals and Rosie were in Rosie's bed. They were all listening to "Mr. Keen, Tracer of Lost Persons" on the radio.

"My God, Rosie," I complained, "how can you survive in this garbage heap?"

"Don't throw my stuff on the floor," she replied. "Put it in the closet."

"You want *me* to hang up the stuff *you* left piled on the bed? You must be crazy."

"Well, don't leave it on the floor. Put it someplace."

I opened the closet door and then I pulled out one of her dresser drawers. There was something very odd about Rosie. Just as messy as was the surface of her room, that's how neat were her drawers and closet. Every pair of underpants, every blouse, every ribbon and barette for her long, thick braids, was folded or arranged as precisely and perfectly as if it were on the shelf at Saks Fifth Avenue. I was just the opposite. I jammed my things into drawers and closets any which way but, if my mother walked into my room, she saw, on the surface, a model of order and discipline.

"I can't put the stuff in here," I said. "I can't just throw it in here. It's too nice. I don't want to mess it up."

Wearily, Rosie climbed out of bed. "All right, all right, I'll do it. Just shut up so I can hear the rest of 'Mr. Keen.' "

I lay down in the other bed and began to read. I was reading *Jane Eyre* for the sixth time. I was very loyal to books I liked. I noticed Dan and Rosie were, too. Dan had read *Treasure Island* twice, though he wasn't as big a reader as Rosie or I. Rosie read *The Wind in the Willows* every spring. I think it was some kind of religious ritual with her. I gave them books on their birthdays, but I had to be careful. I had this way of giving a lecture along with the book. When I did that, they wouldn't read so much as a page of it.

When "Mr. Keen" was over, Rosie switched off the radio and then turned out the lamp on the night table between the two beds. "Hey," I screamed, "what's the big idea? I'm reading." I had just gotten to the part where Mr. Rochester asks Jane what she'll do if he marries Blanche Ingram. I was looking forward to the big love scene which was coming up very soon. I needed that love scene badly. Comfortably and safely, it filled a big hole in my life.

That cut no ice with Rosie. "I want to go to sleep," she said. "I have to get up early."

"So go to sleep," I told her. "I'm not stopping you. Just leave the light on."

"I can't sleep with a light on. You know that." I did know that. It was just one of the reasons I had insisted on moving out of the room two years before, but maybe it was the main one—that and the mess.

"For God's sake, Rosie," I protested, "I can't go to sleep at nine o'clock. Why all of a sudden do you have to go to sleep so early? You're just doing it to annoy me. If I weren't in the room, you'd stay up until midnight."

She didn't get mad at me, or deny what I'd said. She replied simply, "I'm tired. It's my room. I can shut out the light when I want. Go down and read in the lobby if you're not sleepy."

Irrefutable logic again. It was her room and she could do what she wanted in it. That was a rule to which we three had long ago agreed. Even Mother respected that arrangement, which was why Dan's walls were pasted over with pictures of baseball players and jazz musicians. But I didn't want to go down to read in the lobby. I'd have to get dressed to do that, and I certainly didn't feel like getting dressed.

So instead I put on my bathrobe, took my book, and went down the hall to our bathroom. The sign identifying it as a bathroom had been removed from the door, though the holes where the screws had been were still in evidence. It was now our family's private bathroom. Our inn was a fifty-year-old building, originally constructed as an orphanage. Only Room 17, the best room in the house, boasted a private bath that did not open into the hall. Mother had the second-best room, 18, which at least adjoined a bath and, by taking down the sign, she had made it private for us. Even Mr. Jensen didn't use it.

I went in, switched on the light, locked the door, and sat on the toilet. I sat there for an hour, reading. When I got to the part where Jane is living with that insufferable prig, St. John Rivers, my back began to bother me. I shut my book, got up off the toilet, and dragged my cold, aching bones down the hall to Rosie's room. Even the memory of Jane's big clinch with Mr. Rochester wasn't enough to keep me warm. I could think of only one thing—how nice it would be to live in a house, with a proper living room, an easy chair, a standing lamp, and maybe even crocheted antimacassars on the arms of the sofa.

II

In ordinary houses there are pictures on the walls, of course, but they don't usually look anything like the painting my mother dragged home from an auction she went to early Saturday morning at some old farm out in the country.

I was sitting in the lobby, finishing *Jane Eyre*. I read a biography of Charlotte Brönte once. She had a terrible toothache while she was writing *Jane Eyre*. She was almost blind with pain. How could anyone write such a passionate book under circumstances like that? Today she'd go to the dentist every six months for checkups and never experience anything like that toothache. Would that make her more or less of a writer? Or wouldn't it make any difference at all?

I had gotten to the part where Jane leans out of the window and thinks she hears Rochester's voice calling to her, when my mother came into the lobby. It was still early. There was a wedding reception at the Inn that afternoon so Mother couldn't stay away all day. But she loved auctions, and would force herself to get out of bed very early on a Saturday to get to one and still be back in time for whatever was going on at the Inn. She'd look over the merchandise as soon as she arrived and persuade the auctioneer, with whom she was invariably acquainted, to put up for sale the lots in which she was interested before she had to leave. When she and Dad had bought the Inn, it had been furnished in what she derisively described as "Early American Phony," and, ever since, she had been replacing it slowly but steadily with Early American—or English or French—Genuine, purchased at auction sales. She didn't buy any little things which could have been stolen from the Inn—no ash trays or china bowls. Most of the time she purchased only large things, too big to fit into an ordinary sedan.

"What monstrosity did you bring home this time?" I asked, as she came in.

She ignored my sarcasm. "Something marvelous, absolutely marvelous," she said, her eyes shining. "Wait 'til you see it."

"What is it?"

"A picture. For this wall." She pointed to the wide expanse of space opposite the doors which led in from outside. Behind that wall lay her office. Once it had been open, with only the registration counter separating her sanctum from the lobby. She had had it closed in, so at least she could balance cash in private, and had placed a new, small registration desk in the corner to the right of the entrance. But the closed-in, plastered-over archway certainly did need something to finish it off. "Look," she went on, "you go find Sylvester,

Luke, Dan—whoever you can round up. Send them out to help me bring this thing in."

"It must be some picture," I commented.

"Well," she responded, "it'll fill the space. No doubt of that."

In the kitchen I discovered both Luke, the cook, and Sylvester, the porter, who also served as dishwasher when required. Dan I didn't bother to look for. He usually removed himself early on Saturdays to play ball at a friend's house. In the spring and summer it was baseball, in the fall, football, and in the winter, basketball. One form of ball or another was always available to save him from helping out around the place as much as I thought he should.

I accompanied Luke and Sylvester out the back door and around to the front of the building where Mother had parked her 1940 Ford station wagon, which she had bought before the war and was still driving eight years later. The picture was too big to bring in through the kitchen. It had to be carried in through the wide double doors of the front entrance. Mother was standing on the running board, undoing the ropes that tied the painting, wrapped in burlap bags, to the roof. It was too big even for the back of the wagon. It was about eight feet in height and five feet or so in width.

Luke and Sylvester managed to lug the thing through the first set of doors, up the fortunately shallow marble steps of the outer lobby, and through the second set of doors into the building. They half carried, half dragged it across the rubber tile floor and leaned it against the bare wall.

"We're going to need help in hanging it, Mrs. Gold," Luke said. "Sylvester and I won't be able to handle it alone."

Mother glanced at her watch. "Tex'll be here in a little while," she said. "He'll help. And if the three of you can't do it, we'll wait until later, when Mr. Jensen stops by."

"But today's Saturday," I said. "Why would Mr. Jensen come on Saturday?" I'd always thought my room was safe on Saturday.

"Oh, he won't be staying over," Mother reassured me. "He's got so much going on at the plant that he hasn't been able to get to his paper work, so he had to go in today. He's just going to stop by for dinner."

"You're sure?"

Mother looked at me, her eyes narrowed. "Yes," she said, "I'm sure. Don't you believe me?"

"You never can tell," I said softly, "when he'll decide to spend the night."

She didn't answer that one. She just went over to the picture and began to undo its wrappings. Luke and Sylvester helped her. They were done in a few moments. They all stood back then and looked at what they had unveiled.

"Now," my mother said, a wide smile on her face, "isn't he something?"

Luke murmured some kind of agreement. Sylvester didn't say anything, but then he never did. I stared at the thing in front of me for a long minute, and then I turned away. "I don't like him," I said. "He scares me."

26

"I admit he's a little overwhelming at first," Mother allowed, "but you'll see, when he's hung up, he won't loom so large. And he is handsome, don't you think? Did you ever see such a handsome man?"

"I don't think he's handsome at all," I said. "I think he's horrid. He's holding a musket."

"Well, of course," Mother replied. "He's going hunting. I think he looks like a character out of a novel by Sir Walter Scott. Or maybe even like Jane Eyre's Mr. Rochester, in highland dress."

"I don't think so," I disagreed. And yet what she said was not, on the face of it, unreasonable. I'd never pictured Rochester too clearly in my mind. I'd allowed him to remain a shadowy figure. Jane was different. All descriptions to the contrary, Jane looked just like me.

I turned and stared again at the man in the portrait. He stared back at me. I moved a little, but still I could not escape the feeling that he was looking at me. I moved some more, several feet this time, and still his eyes mocked me. I knew that wherever I stood in the lobby it would seem to me that his eyes were on me. I didn't like that.

I didn't like anything else about the man in the picture either. From his dress, he had apparently lived in the late eighteenth or early nineteenth century. For that time, he stood very tall—over six feet. He was middle-aged but, from his carriage and musculature, clearly extremely vigorous. He wore a bright red hunting coat over a brilliant red, white, green, and blue plaid kilt. A sash in a matching plaid went round his shoulder. His hand held, in an upright position, a musket nearly as tall as he was. Behind him was sketched a dim, mountainous landscape. If the picture were cleaned, the highlands might emerge more clearly, but the dust of the years had not much obscured the face.

It was the face that disturbed me. The artist had lit it in such a way that it appeared very strong, actually, to my mind, brutal. The nose was long and thin, the full underlip protruberant, and the blue eyes icy cold. There was a great deal of pride in his look—more than pride, arrogance, rather. I wondered if it were only animals he had hunted with that gun.

Yet there was no doubt that the face was well done. The contrast between light and dark was evidence enough of the artist's skill. The man, I thought, must have actually been proud of the insolence and brutality which I saw in his face. Otherwise he would never have let the artist depict so clearly those aspects of his character.

The painting appeared to be unsigned. It was handsomely framed in carved, gilded wood, and it was the frame that had made it so heavy and awkward to carry. "I got it for a song," Mother said. She was thrilled with her bargain. "It's too big for any ordinary room. Only someone like me, with a hotel lobby, could make use of it. I have no idea where they hung it in that little old farmhouse where the sale was. Or how they acquired it, either. But they had a lot of valuable stuff there. I was only sorry I couldn't stay longer."

"You're not going to hang it here," I protested.

"You're not really going to hang it here where I'll have to pass by it a hundred times a day."

"Of course I am," Mother said. "I bought it just for this wall. It'll be perfect."

"Why don't you put it in the Holiday Room?" I suggested. "I only have to go in there three times a day, for meals, and I can sit with my back to it."

"Oh, Rachel, don't be silly," Mother said. "You'll get used to him. He doesn't look so mean to me. Just dour, like a Scotsman should. Beneath that stern exterior, there beats a heart of gold."

"I see no sign of it, Mother," I said. "I don't like him. I don't like him at all."

"Look at his lips. In a minute he's going to smile."

"No, he won't. If he does, he'll bare his fangs."

"Well, darling," Mother concluded, "you'll learn to live with him."

I shook my head, but I didn't say anything more. Like the time she took a second drink and made me cry, I couldn't explain to her why I was so uncomfortable. I couldn't begin to tell her about all the things that frightened me. She didn't seem to be afraid of anything. But there were times when I wondered if she were really so fearless, or merely insensitive.

Just then Rosie skipped down the stairs and across the lobby. Rosie never walked—she tripped or skipped or danced. She was carrying Buster in her arms. Buster belonged to Mrs. Dunleigh, who lived with her husband, the Major, in Room 17, the best room in the house. Mrs. Dunleigh suffered from a variety of unnamed ailments and, when she didn't feel well enough to walk Buster, she let Rosie do it. Rosie lived for Mrs. Dunleigh's indispositions.

"Well," Mother asked Rosie, "what do you think of him?"

Clutching Buster to her chest, Rosie stared at the painting for a long moment. "I think he's neat," she said at last. "He's so nice and big."

"Rachel doesn't like him," Mother commented. "She thinks he's mean."

"Not to animals," Rosie said.

"Then why is he carrying that gun?" I asked.

"Just decoration," Rosie informed me.

I lost. By mid-afternoon, the portrait was properly hung on the wall. Of course, there had never been any question that Mother would do as she pleased about it. If she had been even slightly inclined to doubt her choice, the general admiration the painting elicited that evening would have laid any reservations to rest. But she hadn't had them in the first place. She never did. And when she asked someone what he or she thought about a certain matter, what she was seeking was not an opinion but ratification.

The following week, she was surer than ever that the painting was one of the cleverest purchases she'd ever made. Late Friday afternoon a man from New York came to stay for the weekend. I was in the lobby reading when I heard his footsteps on the tile floor. "Can I help you?" I asked, as I got up from my chair and moved toward him.

He was dressed in a fine-looking, fur-collared camel hair coat. As a matter of fact, he was a fine-looking man in general, about fifty-five, with a gray handlebar mustache and bushy gray eyebrows. "I'd like a room for the weekend," he said, "with a private bath, please."

"I'm sorry," I replied, glancing into the key box on the wall behind the registration desk, "all the rooms with private baths are occupied. But I can give you a very nice room with a sink, right next to the bath. Everything is very clean."

He glanced around the lobby, meanwhile breathing in deeply through his nose. He was giving the Waterbridge Inn the smell test. I didn't mind. I knew we'd pass. "It looks clean enough," he admitted. "All right. The room with a sink will do." He signed the registration card with his own fountain pen. "Augustus Stoner," he wrote, "Stoner Antiques, 720 Madison Ave., New York." Then he paid me for both nights in advance, without my asking. We always collected room rents in advance; otherwise, transients had the unfortunate habit of skipping out very, very early in the morning, before anyone was awake to collect their money, sometimes taking the blankets and towels with them.

"I'll ring for the porter," I said, pushing down the stem of the little bell that was fixed to the counter top. "He'll show you to your room, and carry your bag."

"Thank you," Mr. Stoner nodded, and then his eyes once again moved around the room. "You have many fine-looking pieces here," he said. "Are any of them for sale?"

"I don't know," I said. "You'd have to ask my mother." I didn't imagine she'd be adverse to making a profit on some of the things she'd bought at her auctions if the opportunity presented itself.

"Family pieces?" he asked.

I had to smile at the thought of my grandparents dragging all that furniture across the ocean with them in the steerage compartments of steamships fifty years before. "No," I replied. "She got them at sales, out in the country. Hunterdon County, mostly."

"Ah," he smiled. "I'm here myself for one at the Dalton estate tomorrow, in Tewkesbury Township. Perhaps, if she's going, I can go with her. Otherwise, I'm sure I'll lose my way."

"No," I replied, "I don't think she's going. We have a very busy day here at the Inn tomorrow, and I heard her say that one'll be too rich for her blood anyhow. She only buys if she can get a fantastic bargain."

His hand stroked the bell. "She has a good eye," he said. She did, and so did he. The bell was solid brass and had been cast in 1870, over seventy-five years before. That's why it was bolted to the counter top.

Sylvester came then to take Mr. Stoner and his bag upstairs. My mother always wanted to know about everyone who came in and out of the Waterbridge Inn, so I went into her office to report the latest arrival. She was pleased when I told her he'd said she had a good eye. Later, when he came down to dinner, I introduced them.

"Mother," I said, standing there between them with

32

my lumpy arms hanging at my side, "this is the antique dealer I told you about. Mr. Stoner."

"Bea Gold," my mother said, extending her hand gracefully. "I'm happy to meet you, Mr. Stoner."

"Augustus, please," Mr. Stoner said, looking directly into her eyes as he took her hand. For a second I thought he was actually going to raise it to his lips and kiss it.

"Well, then, Augustus," Mother said, smiling that dazzling smile of hers which blinded anyone who met her, male or female, to the fact that she was short and thick-waisted, that her hair was too fine, her noise too long, and her eyes too small.

"Your daughter tells me you won't be able to go to the Dalton sale tomorrow," Mr. Stoner said. "That's truly a pity. Don't you think you could break away for a little while? I'd love company."

"Oh, I wish I could," Mother said, with a regretful little sigh, "but with you there, and all the other dealers, what chance would I have? I would go anyway, just to see the place, if I weren't going to be so busy. But this time it's impossible—just impossible."

"I hope I might have the pleasure of your company another day, then," Mr. Stoner suggested.

"That would be *my* pleasure," Mother said. "I could learn so much from you. Would you care for a drink before dinner?" It appeared that my mother found Mr. Stoner quite as charming as he found her.

"That would be very nice," Mr. Stoner said.

"We'll have it here, in the lobby," Mother decided.

33

"There are no antiques to look at in the bar. It's all new—chrome and blue leather. What would you like?"

"A dry martini would be nice," Mr. Stoner said.

"Tell Tex to bring it in here, would you please, Rachel?" Mother asked. "And a scotch sour for me." I was dismissed.

I went to the bar and ordered the drinks from Tex. I couldn't carry them out because I was only sixteen and it was against the law for anyone under twenty-one to serve liquor. I went back out into the lobby and saw that Major and Mrs. Dunleigh had joined my mother and Mr. Stoner. I don't know how much Mother cared for that—she considered Mrs. Dunleigh a silly woman—but there wasn't much she could do about it. The Inn was a public place. Since she was stuck with the Dunleighs anyway, I presumed there'd be no objection to me. I took a chair next to the small sofa on which Mother and Mr. Stoner were seated. When Tex came with the drinks, the Major ordered a bourbon and soda for himself and a glass of sherry for his wife.

"Oh, I don't want anything," Mrs. Dunleigh protested.

"I'll do you good," the Major said. "Perk up your appetite."

"All right, then" she agreed, her voice heavy with resignation. "But I still don't think it'll do any good," she added softly.

The Major didn't even hear her. "So you're an antique dealer, are you, Stoner?" he asked heartily. "Any money to be made in that business?"

"I have no complaints," Mr. Stoner replied drily.

"Like anything else," the Major went on, "it's a question of buying cheap and selling dear."

"As you say, Major," Mr. Stoner responded politely. But then he directed his attention exclusively to my mother. "Do you ever think of parting with any of the items you've collected?"

Tex came then and served Major and Mrs. Dunleigh. Even though I hadn't asked, he brought a Coke for me.

"Well, anything's for sale, if the price is right," Mother responded to Mr. Stoner. "What are you interested in?"

"The ladderback chair," he replied casually. "The brass bell. The cherry drop-leaf table. That painting." With his head, he nodded in the direction of the portrait. I usually passed it with eyes averted but, now that Mr. Stoner was gesturing toward it, I could not help turning my head in the direction his finger was pointing. The handsome face with its cold blue eyes stared back at me with a sneer.

"I imagine its mere size makes that picture worth something," my mother replied. "But that very same size also limits its usefulness."

"That's true," Mr. Stoner replied, judiciously stroking the end of his mustache. "But I think it's worth more than something. It's beautifully done."

"Is it?" Mother queried. "I know I like it. But then I know nothing about painting. I've tried to learn a little about furniture and china and, of course, I love jewelry. But painting is a mystery to me."

"Is it signed?" Mr. Stoner asked. Mother shook her head. "No writing on the other side?" he continued. "No paper stuck behind the backing?"

"I didn't see anything," Mother replied. "That doesn't mean nothing's there, however. I didn't take the backing off."

"No, that would have been a lot of trouble in a painting so large," Mr. Stoner went on. His eyes were fixed on the portrait as he spoke. "Just because you didn't see a signature doesn't mean one isn't there. It's my opinion that the picture is a portrait of Sir Baldwin MacClough. He was Laird of Waterbridge in the late 1700s."

"Why, how marvelous," Mother cried. "How appropriate! What an incredible coincidence that a portrait of the Laird of Waterbridge should end up in Waterbridge, New Jersey!"

I saw we'd never be rid of the damn thing now. "How do you know it's Sir Baldwin MacClough?" I interrupted.

"He's wearing the MacClough tartan," Mr. Stoner replied, a certain note of self-congratulation in his voice. "I know enough about Scotch tartans to know that. The cut of his coat, that old musket, and the style of the painting too make it clear that we're looking at a portrait done about 1800, give or take a few years either way. And he certainly doesn't look like he's second in command." I had to agree to that. "I happen to have a pretty fair knowledge of the British peerage," Mr. Stoner went on. "It's necessary in my business. So if I see a portrait of a very imposing figure in the dress of the late eighteenth century, and if his plaid marks him as a MacClough, I say to myself, 'Ergo, Sir Baldwin MacClough, Laird of Waterbridge.'" I would not have been surprised if he had added, "Elementary, my dear Watson." But instead he said, "It's not so strange that the Laird of Waterbridge would end up in Waterbridge, New Jersey. This is an old town, and there must be a reason why it has the name it has."

"I didn't get it in Waterbridge," Mother said. "I got it out in Neshanic Station."

"Yes, yes," Mr. Stoner interrupted impatiently. "I know that. But you got it near here. Near enough." Then he smiled, as if to apologize for his sudden shortness. "I don't know as much about the history of New Jersey as I do about the British peerage. If you investigated, you might find that the whole area was once called Waterbridge, and it wasn't until later that the name was limited to one town. That used to happen all the time."

"I'm really glad to know who he is," Mother said, gazing thoughtfully into Sir Baldwin's eyes. "Knowing makes him even more precious to me. It would take a great deal of money to make me part with him now." She turned her face back toward Mr. Stoner. "But, just as a matter of curiosity, what do you think I could get for him?"

Mr. Stoner glanced at her with a speculative look in his eye. I was sure he thought she was trying to see what sort of price he himself would give her for the picture but, if that was what she was doing, he, as a businessman, seemed to think no less of her for it. However, he made himself perfectly clear. "I wouldn't buy it unless I had a customer for it," he said. "As you say, it's not for everyone. But the right party, well, the right party might give you as much as a thousand for it. Let's say a hotel or a club in the city, or even a descendant of Sir Baldwin's. There are many, I understand, from both sides of the sheets, and some of them are rich."

Major Dunleigh shook his head in amazement. "Unbelievable," he said. "A thousand dollars for some paint and a piece of canvas."

"And a great deal of talent," Mr. Stoner interjected sharply. "Look at the fluent, blunt brushwork, so appropriate for that craggy Scotch face." But the Major merely shook his head again.

"Well, if you find a customer," I announced, "do come back for it, Mr. Stoner."

"Of course, for enough money, anything's for sale," my mother said. "For enough money, this whole place is for sale. But I don't really want to sell the picture. It's so appropriate here. It belongs here."

Mr. Stoner nodded his agreement. "We're just speculating anyway," he said. "It's one thing to name a price and another thing to get it." Then he added quickly, "I get a ten percent agent's fee when I sell something I don't own myself."

Mother smiled. "Of course. That's only fair. But I'm not selling it."

"Not now, anyway," Mr. Stoner said.

Late the next afternoon, I was coming down the stairs when I saw Mr. Stoner alone in the otherwise empty lobby. The Dalton sale was over, I supposed. He didn't see me. He was absorbed in what he was doing—closely examining the bottom of the portrait of Sir Baldwin with a magnifying glass. Perhaps he was looking for a signature. Occupied as he was, he nevertheless heard the door of my mother's private office creak as she came out into the lobby. Before she saw him, he dropped the glass into his pocket and turned away from the picture. Then I came the rest of the way down the stairs and stood at the bottom, listening to them.

"Ah, Augustus," Mother said. "Did you have a successful day? Was it a good sale?"

"Not bad," Mr. Stoner replied pleasantly. "I picked up a few things. Have dinner with me and I'll tell you about them."

"I really shouldn't . . ." Mother hesitated. "It's Saturday night."

"I'll wait," Mr. Stoner said. "I'll wait until things quiet down. I'm in no hurry. I'll have a few more of Tex's delicious dry martinis and read while I'm waiting."

"It won't be before nine," Mother warned.

"The hours will fly by if I know that time with you is at the end of them," Mr. Stoner replied gallantly.

Mother laughed. "Are you sure you're an antique

dealer?" she teased. "You sound more like a Lothario."

"The two are not necessarily mutually exclusive," Mr. Stoner assured her.

I heard no more. I went into the kitchen to get my own dinner. I suppose they did dine together, later. But the next morning, Sunday, he was gone early, before any of the rest of us were up.

III

A few days later, after she got done at the hairdresser's, Mother picked me up at school. We were going downtown to buy the dress she'd promised me for Sally's party.

"You ever going to get a new car?" I asked her, as I sat down next to her on a worn, brown leather seat from the seams of which pale, soiled tufts of stuffing were beginning to emerge.

"Maybe next year, if all's well," she said. "This one's still OK. After all, during the war, with gas rationing, I didn't use it very much." It's not that my mother was stingy. It's just that she had a limited amount of money and she spent it on what was important to her. Besides her antiques, which she regarded as a business investment, she liked good jewelry, and she liked coats. She must have owned ten coats, all cloth. She didn't care about fur coats, and she didn't care about cars. She thought a car was to get you where you wanted to go and, as long as it did that, you didn't need a new one. I think the coat thing was psychological. Between the Depression and the war, she once went ten years without a new coat. When business improved with the war, the first thing she did when she had some money was buy a new coat. And the second and the third things, too.

We went into La Mode. Mrs. Littnauer waited on us. She and Mr. Littnauer owned La Mode, but she did all the work. She did the buying and a lot of the selling. He just sat behind the register all day and took cash—a big, pale blob, whom I had never seen once move off the stool.

Mrs. Littnauer must have brought thirty dresses back to the fitting room for me to try on. But most of them weren't right on me. I was sixteen years old and a size sixteen, not, after all, a very promising combination. There was one rose velvet thing with a white lace collar and cuffs, cut in a princess line, which didn't look bad, but there was nothing at all sophisticated about it. When I was seven, I'd had one just like it, only blue, handed down from Aunt Faye's daughter, Cousin Stephanie. "Put me in a pair of Mary Janes and I'll look like a five-year-old from Brobdingnag," I said.

"Brobdingnag?" Mrs. Littnauer peered at me over her glasses. "Where's that?"

"Near Parsippany," I replied.

"Well, that's New Jersey," Mrs. Littnauer said. "I thought I knew pretty nearly every town in New Jersey."

"Rachel is teasing you, Stella," my mother explained. "Brobdingnag is a land of giants in a book, *Gulliver's Travels.*"

"I've heard of that book," Mrs. Littnauer said, blinking her eyes nervously, "but I thought it was about little people."

"Oh, it is, it is," Mother reassured her. "Only it has another section, too, about giants."

"And another one about horses," I added. "Maybe that's what I am, a horse."

"Stop talking nonsense, Rachel," my mother scolded. She couldn't stand it when any of us expressed doubts about ourselves. In her perfect confidence, she had no patience with self-doubt, particularly in her children to whom, as a matter of course, her own perfection should extend.

Mrs. Littnauer was more sympathetic. "I have something that may look lovely on you," she said. "It just came in. We haven't even tagged it yet." She left the dressing room and came back a few minutes later with a dress of black silk.

"Black?" my mother asked doubtfully. "She's only sixteen."

"Wait 'til she puts it on," Mrs. Littnauer said. "You'll see. The cut is very youthful."

So I tried the dress on and, of course, because it was black, I actually looked thin in it. Also, because it was black, no one could imagine that I was a five-year-old giant. The bodice was fitted, the skirt was full and fell almost to my ankles in what was referred to as the "New Look," and, best of all, it was off-the-shoulder, revealing what was no doubt my best point—probably my only good one—my smooth, white neck and shoulders. "It's beautiful," I said. I looked down at the price tag. "Twenty-two fifty," I read. "Oh Lord, is that too much?"

"We can manage it," Mother said, "if we like the dress."

"We do like it, don't we?" I urged, remembering the bargain. She had to like it, too.

"Oh, yes," Mother said. "I do like it. You look beautiful in it. But black . . ."

"Mother, I love this dress." Then I added the clincher. "I love me in this dress."

"Well," Mother agreed, "that's the important thing about a dress—that you feel good when you're wearing it."

"Oh, I do, I do," I said. "I've never felt so good in my life."

"You can borrow my pearls," Mother said. "Pearls are nice on young girls. Really, it'll be marvelous if we can settle on something right here in Waterbridge. I just don't have time to go to New Brunswick or Plainfield this weekend."

"You won't find anything nicer than what we have here in New Brunswick or Plainfield," Mrs. Littnauer said, "or in Newark, either. We carry the same lines as Bamberger's."

"And you have much nicer sales people," Mother added, with a smile. Mrs. Littnauer was placated. She put the dress in a box, tied it with a string, and handed it to me. I carried it out of the store like a trophy.

We drove home through the lowering twilight. As we came up the long gravel drive that led to the Inn, we could see that Luke, or Min, or someone, had re-membered to turn on the huge neon signs that stood on the roof of the square stucco building. The signs said "WATERBRIDGE INN." One faced east and the other faced west, and they could be seen for miles down the highway. But the electricity in some of the letters was always out. The building was old, and the wiring wasn't what it should have been. The high winds that frequently hit the roof didn't help, either. That night one sign read "ATE BRID E," while the other said "AT RIDGE INN."

"Oh, damn," Mother said, when she noticed them. "I have to call the electrician again. He's here every other week."

"Why don't you just give up on those signs?" I asked. "They're so green and ugly anyway."

"But they're a landmark," Mother defended them. "Even when they're half out, everyone knows what they mean."

When we got inside the building, Mother went straight to her office to do her books. Rosie was sitting in the lobby, talking to Mrs. Dunleigh and Buster. Rosie was always talking to someone—one of the guests or one of the help. They all seemed to love her, and she them. She was still young enough for her plumpness to be considered cute, and she had freckles and long, thick braids. She was the only one of the three of us who had inherited our father's large, thick-lashed, deep blue eyes.

"Well, I think Boston terriers are just lovely," Rosie was saying, "but I like poodles and Scotties, too."

"Scotties were nothing before Roosevelt became president," Mrs. Dunleigh said. "They became popular just because he had one."

"Well, I don't like Scotties because of President Roosevelt," Rosie said. "I like them because they're small. My mother says an inn is no place for a dog, so I think I have more chance of talking her into a small one than a big one. Don't you?"

Before Mrs. Dunleigh could reply, I said, "You've got no chance of talking her into any kind of dog at all. You want to come upstairs and help me try on my new dress?"

"No," Rosie replied, "I don't. I want to stay here and talk about dogs with Mrs. Dunleigh and Buster."

Just then Mr. Jensen came into the building and walked over to the registration desk. As usual, I was able to contain my enthusiasm at the sight of him. Another, much younger man was with him. Rosie saw them, too, and immediately forgot all about Mrs. Dunleigh and Buster as she ran across the lobby to greet Mr. Jensen. Rosie loved Mr. Jensen. It wasn't she who got thrown out of her bed for his sake. I guess Mr. Jensen loved Rosie, too. After he hugged her, I saw him reach into his pocket and pull out a tiny box which he gave her. He always had something in his pocket for Rosie, even if it was only a piece of candy. She was so anxious to be treated like a grown-up and put the gravy on the turkey when we helped Luke serve a banquet, you'd think she'd have gotten over being a little girl so far as Mr. Jensen and some of the other customers were concerned. But I noticed that

Rosie liked to play it both ways. She was the baby when it was to her advantage; she was almost-eleven when that suited her better.

I picked up my dress box and started across the lobby toward the stairs when Mr. Jensen called me. "Rachel, come here a second." I turned and went back toward the registration desk. I guess my face wasn't exactly alight with warmth and friendliness, because Mr. Jensen said right away, "Don't worry, I'm not sleeping in your room tonight. Jeff and I have number 14. I want you to know I really appreciate it when you give me your room. I know it's inconvenient for you. I'll make it up to you one day, you can be sure."

"That's OK," I mumbled, with what little grace I could muster. "Do you know for sure you've got number 14 tonight?" I added, as I stepped behind the counter.

"Yes," Mr. Jensen said. "I spoke to your mother on the phone this morning."

I pushed the tray holding the pen and registration cards toward him. I took keys out of the box labelled "14" and laid them on the counter.

"By the way, Rachel," Mr. Jensen said, as he signed the card, "this is Jeff." He waved his head toward the young man standing next to him. "Jeff will be working with me for the next several weeks. He lives in New York, so I guess you'll be seeing a good deal of him, too, when we have to stay late at the plant."

"Hello, Rachel," Jeff said. I looked up at him and smiled. I couldn't help smiling. He had freckles all over his face, like Rosie, and a thick thatch of red hair.

47

He was about the pleasantest-looking person I'd ever seen.

"Hello, Jeff," I replied. I picked up one of the keys off the counter and held it out to him. "Here's your key."

He took it from my hand. "Thanks," he said, as his fingers brushed my palm.

I could see a leather suitcase resting on the floor next to him. All Mr. Jensen had with him was a briefcase. "Shall I call Sylvester to carry your bag up for you?"

"No, thanks," Jeff said. "I can manage. It's not heavy."

Mr. Jensen had finished filling out the registration card. He took his key and gestured to Jeff to follow him. "Thanks, Rachel," he said. "See you later, Rosie," he added, giving her head a pat. He and Jeff crossed the lobby and disappeared up the stairs.

"What did he give you?" I asked Rosie.

"A birthday present," Rosie replied. "He said not to open it until December 8."

"You're not going to listen to him, are you?" I asked.

"Of course I am," Rosie said. "What would be the point of opening it today?"

I could not imagine such willpower. "How did he know your birthday was coming?" I asked. He'd never given me a birthday present, and it was my room he slept in.

"I told him," Rosie replied simply. "Last time he was here I told him. I think he's rich."

"Don't be disappointed," I said, "if there's something less than a diamond ring in that box."

"Oh, I *know* what's in the box," Rosie replied. "I told him what I wanted."

"Oh, my God, Rosie," I exclaimed. "You're impossible." But my curiosity triumphed over my disapproval. "What is it?"

"It's not a diamond ring," she said smugly. "It's a turquoise ring. Turquoise is my birthstone."

"You're a con artist, Rosie," I said, feeling equal parts of admiration and dismay. "Do you think it's very nice of you to wheedle Mr. Jensen into buying you a turquoise ring?"

"He asked me what I wanted and I told him," Rosie replied. "I really don't see what's wrong with that. He didn't have to buy it if he didn't want to."

"Maybe it isn't a turquoise ring at all," I said. "Maybe it's two pumpkin seeds."

"Maybe it is," Rosie agreed. "We won't know until my birthday." She ran off then to Mrs. Dunleigh and Buster, kneeling down beside the poor asthmatic creature and petting him as passionately as if he were the prize dog in the Westminster Kennel Club show.

I went into the office to tell my mother about the new arrivals. "Mr. Jensen brought a young man with him," I informed her. "A Jeff Dulac."

"Yes," Mother said. "He told me he would, over the phone. This Jeff Dulac is on some kind of consulting job at Jensen Tool and Die. He'll be a good customer."

"For a while," I retorted suddenly. "Sooner or later, even the regulars disappear, and we never hear from them again. Even the help leaves. Just when you get to really caring about them, they leave."

Mother looked up from her cashbook. "Change is the law of life," she said quietly.

"On the other hand," I protested, "some things don't change fast enough!"

"Like what?" Mother asked.

"Like fat, funny-looking me!"

Mother snorted. "You're extremely good-looking. All my children are." I expected her to add, "I wouldn't have it any other way," but she said, instead, "If you think you're too heavy, lose some weight."

"Easier said than done," I muttered.

"If there's one thing I can't bear," Mother scolded, "it's self-pity, particularly from one who has no reason to pity herself. Are you crippled? Are you stupid? Are you hungry, or ill-clothed? If you were, then you'd have something to gripe about. You're fatherless, it's true, but then I'm husbandless. Somehow, we manage."

I shrugged and walked out of the office. She was perfect. What can you say to someone who's perfect?

I tried not to look at the portrait of Sir Baldwin Mac-Clough when I was in the lobby but, in spite of my distaste for him, there was something about him that fascinated me, and I often found my eyes drawn to his, as if against my conscious will. This was one of those times. I looked up at him. "She's just like you are," I told him silently. "You both think you know everything!"

Then I went upstairs to try on my new dress.

IV

The Tuesday before Thanksgiving did not go down in my book as among the ten best days of the year. It was one of those dreary, damp, mean November days that give New Jersey a bad name. I had to stay after school to make up a chemistry test I'd missed when I'd been out with a cold. Makeup tests were always much harder than the original tests and, since the material had been taught a month before, I'd forgotten most of it anyway. My secret love, Billy Colbert, had to make up the same test.

Afterward, we left the chemistry lab together. "Well, it was long," Billy said, "but it wasn't hard."

"I thought it was long *and* hard," I replied.

"Oh, cut it out, Rachel," Billy remonstrated. "If there's one thing I can't stand, it's brains who pretend they suffer just as much as the rest of us."

"I'm not a brain in chemistry," I protested. "If I get good grades in science or math, it's because I work. You're the brain in chemistry. I hate that word, brain, anyway. Everyone has a brain, and they're all about the same size, even a moron's."

We walked past the gym. The cheerleaders were just coming out of practice. Football season was nearly over, but they had to cheer at basketball games, too. Sometimes they even had to cheer at wrestling matches. They didn't like that very much because there were hardly any spectators at wrestling matches.

"Hey, Bill!" Tess Galaini called, as she caught sight of us. "Going over to Ginty's? Wait for me!" Tess and Billy had gone steady in eighth grade and ever since, when they were between romances, like now, they took up with each other. "You, too," Tess said to me, in what was obviously an afterthought. "You come, too." As my lab partner she depended upon my good will. Every morning in homeroom she copied my chemistry assignment.

I seldom went to Ginty's, where the athletes and the cheerleaders and their satellites hung out. But I was thirsty, and it was a chance to be with Billy for a little while, so I said OK. We accompanied Tess to her locker and then the three of us walked the short block to Main Street and Ginty's Sweet Shop. On the way I said very little. Mostly Billy and Tess talked to each other. "Lord, I really am thirsty," Tess said. "I need something after all that dumb jumping around and screaming."

"Why, Tess," Billy said, with exaggerated surprise, "aren't you just crazy about being a cheerleader?"

"Oh, I love it," she responded derisively. "All this rah-rah stuff is for infants. I'm sick of it." I could hardly believe my ears. How could anyone get sick of being part of the most prestigious group of females in the school? I mean, in my own thoughts, I could make fun of cheerleading as a mindless activity, but I couldn't sneer at the popularity and adoration the cheerleaders received as their due. I couldn't be that dishonest with myself. "If you don't like it," I asked Tess, "why do you do it?"

She tossed her head, and her shoulder-length blonde pageboy bounced smartly and then settled back perfectly into place. "I don't know how to get out of it, especially now that they've elected me captain. It's all so boring." Did she mean that? I couldn't know.

When we got to Ginty's Sweet Shop, Billy held the door open for us. Tess entered first, and I followed her into the steamy, smoke-filled interior. Since I was not an habitué of the place, I found myself trailing rather uncomfortably behind Tess as she made her way toward the back, exchanging raucous greetings with inhabitants of the booths as she went.

There was no empty table. Without any hesitation at all, Tess halted her royal progress at one occupied by another cheerleader, a sophomore whom I knew only as Missy, and Carl Hessle, a loudmouthed boor I couldn't stand. "Sit down," Tess ordered, and I had no choice but to slide into the seat opposite Missy and Carl, pushing myself all the way over against the wall to make room for Tess and Billy.

"We did OK today, don't you think?" Missy asked Tess. "We finally got the choo-choo cheer down pat."

Tess's eyes flicked coolly over Missy. "I don't know how we did," she said. "It's all a lot of crap."

"Cheerleading?" Missy's bland blue eyes grew wide with dismay. "Cheerleading?"

53

"Well, the choo-choo cheer isn't the Lord's Prayer," Tess said. "It isn't sacred."

Carl laughed. "You're spending too much time in that lab with Rachel," he told Tess. Carl and I always argued in history class. I regarded him as a fascist, scarcely a cut above Hitler, and he thought I made Henry Wallace look like William Howard Taft. But, though I found it easy enough to counter Carl's remarks in class, in this setting I was without a single witty response, even to a sophomore like Missy, let alone Carl.

Several sticky, empty Coke bottles remained uncleared on the table. Since I had nothing to say, I picked up one of the empty bottles and began to play with it.

"If you don't care about cheerleading, you shouldn't have accepted the captaincy," Missy said angrily. "You shouldn't even be on the squad," she added, her pink face flushed with emotion.

Tess merely raised her eyebrows. "Why don't you impeach me?" she suggested.

"Calm down, Missy," Billy said. "It isn't important."

Missy lowered her voice obediently at Billy's command, but she continued scolding Tess. "If it isn't important, I'd like to know what is. The trouble with you juniors is that you haven't got any school spirit any more." She ranted on, and I, having no way of changing the subject, continued playing idiotically with the Coke bottle. I stuck my fat finger down the neck of the bottle. It was a tight fit, I realized immediately, and, with the uncomfortable sensation beginning to form that I had done a foolish thing, I tried to pull my finger out of the bottle neck. It wouldn't come. I moved the entire apparatus onto my lap, and continued to struggle with it there. But the more I tugged, the tighter my index finger seemed wedged into that bottle.

It was Tess who noticed something was the matter. "For heaven's sake, Rachel," she asked, "what're you doing down there on your lap?"

I put my Coke bottle and its finger back on the table. "I seem to have surpassed even my customary clumsiness," I muttered. My embarrassment was so great that I wanted to jump up from the table and run away, but how could I pass through Ginty's and out into the street with a Coke bottle dangling from my finger?

Carl grabbed the bottle and began to pull at it. I thought my finger was going to fall out of my hand, but the bottle didn't budge. "Stop it, Carl," I said. "You're hurting me."

"Perhaps if you ran it under cold water . . ." Tess suggested.

"Yes," I replied. "That's a good idea." Why hadn't I thought of that? But then I did think of something. "Everyone will see this stupid thing . . ." My voice trailed off. I didn't care to admit I feared being laughed at.

"Drape your coat over your arm," Tess said matter-of-factly.

I stood up, grabbed my coat from the hook, and hung it over my arm. Luckily, the ladies' room was empty. I ran the bottle and my finger under cold water and, in a minute, was able to release the finger without any difficulty at all. I threw the offending bottle into the garbage pail. I thought, Let Mr. Ginty find it there if he wants to collect the deposit. His help should do a better job of clearing tables between customers, that was all.

I put on my coat and marched out of the ladies' room, looking neither to the right nor left. When I passed the table where Tess, Missy, Billy, and Carl were sitting, I saw that they were giggling. Probably at me, I decided. I said the shortest possible of good-byes, and walked past the table. "Rache . . ." Tess called after me. I pretended I didn't hear her and got myself out of Ginty's as quickly as I could. It served me right, the whole business, for going where I didn't belong. I had been better off when I was Rosie's age, content to bury my head in a book and blissfully unaware of the opposite sex.

Things weren't any better when I got home. I was exhausted by the time I'd completed the long walk to the Inn in the early November dark. Though it wasn't yet five o'clock, the green neon sign on the roof was already lit. I walked through the doors into the lobby to be greeted by the sneering, staring eyes of Sir Baldwin MacClough. He seemed to know I'd gotten my finger stuck in a Coke bottle. "To hell with you, Sir Nasty," I muttered under my breath. "You're all alike, you men." Fortunately, no one else was in the lobby to hear me.

But before I could get upstairs, my mother came out of her office. "Rachel," she called, as soon as she saw me, "where've you been?"

"I told you, Mother, I had to stay after school to make up a chemistry test."

"Yes," she remembered, "I suppose you did." It was perfectly normal for Mother not to recall what one of us had told her, but she usually didn't worry much about our comings and goings, so long as we ate supper at the Inn, or told her if we weren't going to. She made Rosie cross the highway before dark. She had made Dan and me do the same when we were younger. But, otherwise, I think she was just as pleased if we kept ourselves occupied after school and on weekends. As she always said, she trusted us. She couldn't have managed her life if she hadn't. And we never betrayed her trust—Dan because he hadn't thought of it yet, Rosie because she was too young, and I because I was afraid.

But tonight she wanted me home, and it wasn't because she was worried about me. "Go help Rosie," she ordered. "She's upstairs trying to make up the rooms all by herself. Olga's sick and never showed up today, and I've just been too busy to get to them." Olga was the chambermaid.

"Oh, God," I moaned, and threw my books down on the worn, maroon leather sofa nearest me. "That's all I need today, that's all I need. Twenty-two beds to make up. Seventeen rooms and four bathrooms to clean."

"Number 14 was empty last night," Mother replied, taking no notice whatsoever of my snit. "You can skip Rosie's room, and Dan's, and yours. But you'd better get started on the rest of them. It's getting late. They're all rented for tonight."

I picked up my books and headed for the stairs.

"Where's Dan?" I called back to her. "He can help, too."

"I don't know where Dan is," she answered. "He hasn't come home yet."

"It isn't fair," I protested. "He never does anything."

She paused by the double doorway that led into the Holiday Room and turned to look at me across the wide expanse of the lobby. "You sound like Rosie," she said. "I wouldn't expect to hear something like that from someone your age."

"I hate this place," I said, in a loud, clear voice she would have been able to hear all the way in the kitchen. "I hate it." And then I whirled around and marched up the stairs.

It took Rosie and me an hour and a half to do the rooms. We had to change the bed linen on all the beds, bring in fresh towels, empty the wastebaskets, and wipe out the sinks. We didn't bother to vacuum unless we could actually see loose dirt on the rug, and we didn't dust at all. Olga would probably be back tomorrow, and things like vacuuming and dusting could be skipped for one day. At least, that's what we thought.

I was in such a foul mood that Rosie stopped speaking to me altogether. Since I jumped down her throat every time she opened her mouth, I could scarcely blame her. We tramped from room to room in silence, knocking at each door before we put the master key in the lock and entered. So late in the day, some of the regulars might already be in. That would be unfortunate. It's not pleasant to arrive home after a day's work and find your room a mess, and a customer might rightfully complain about such a situation. Luckily, no one responded to our knocks until we hit Room 17, where Major and Mrs. Dunleigh lived, with Buster.

Major Dunleigh opened the door for us. "Well," he said, his glance taking in our pail and cleanser, our piles of sheets and towels, "it's about time someone made up this room."

"Yes, Major," I apologized. "I'm sorry. Olga didn't come in today." I scurried into the bathroom, and left Rosie to deal with the beds. Since she got on well with Mrs. Dunleigh, the Dunleighs wouldn't scold her the way they might me. You'd have to be inhuman to yell at a ten-year-old with freckles and braids who was struggling to put clean sheets on your bed.

Sure enough, when I came back into the room, I found Mrs. Dunleigh helping her. The Major sat in the armchair reading *The Saturday Evening Post*, and Buster sat on the floor whining softly at the sight of Mrs. Dunleigh's unaccustomed flurry of activity. She walked him for a couple of miles each morning, but that was about all she ever did. "I think this is a lot of work for a little girl," Mrs. Dunleigh said to Rosie. "I think it's wonderful of you to help out your mother this way."

"Yes," Rosie agreed complacently, "it is very nice of me. But look at it this way. Most days, I don't even have to make my own bed so, if once a month I have to make twenty beds, it comes out even. I really don't end up doing any more than any other girl my age."

"When I was a little girl in Baltimore," Mrs. Dunleigh said, "I never had to make a bed. We always had a cook and a housekeeper, and an upstairs maid, and a man for the yard."

"You were rich," Rosie said.

"Not really rich," Mrs. Dunleigh replied. "It's just that Mama and Papa always wanted everything right, everything proper."

Major Dunleigh slammed his magazine down on the table next to his easy chair and stood up. "I'm going down to the bar," he announced. "I need a drink."

Mrs. Dunleigh didn't seem to hear him. She went right on talking to Rosie. "And, of course," she said, "they had enough money for that. They had enough money to do things right. We always dressed for dinner and sat in the dining room. The table was polished so bright you could see your face in it, and there was always a big bowl of fresh flowers and two tall white candles in the middle."

"Even when you didn't have company?" Rosie asked. She sounded as if she were really interested. "Even when there was just the three of you?"

"Four of us," Mrs. Dunleigh corrected. "I had a little brother. Didn't I ever tell you about my little brother Abel?"

"No," Rosie said, "you never did."

"Well," Mrs. Dunleigh began, "it was terribly sad . . . the saddest thing that ever happened to us, you know. Abel was born, let's see . . . it must have been in 1903. That's right—if he were alive today, he'd be 45 years old, five years younger than I am . . . ."

It was obvious that Mrs. Dunleigh could go on all night. Number 17 was the last room we had to do. I put some clean towels in the bathroom, gathered up the

dirty linen and our equipment, and started out of the
room. "I'll see you later, Rosie," I said. "Good night,
Mrs. Dunleigh."

"Yeah," Rosie said, not really withdrawing her rapt
attention from Mrs. Dunleigh, who didn't notice my
departure any more than she'd noticed her husband's.

What an actress Rosie was. She didn't give a darn
about Mrs. Dunleigh's Baltimore childhood, or the
poor, dead baby brother. All she cared about was Buster.
She figured if she hung around long enough, Mrs. Dunleigh would let her take Buster out for his evening
walk, and then she'd go back in the fields behind the
Inn and try to get that poor, asthmatic, aging Boston
terrier to run. She was trying to turn him back into a
real dog. I had to admire Rosie. She wasn't likely ever
to get her finger stuck in a bottle.

In the hall I met Jeff Dulac. He was carrying a very
large suitcase. He paused when he saw me, and set it
down. "Hi, Rachel," he said. "You the maid today?"

"Yes," I replied, as I dumped the dirty linen into a
big laundry bag. "Olga's sick. I'm done now, thank
goodness." I looked up into his cheerful, open face with
its blue eyes and crooked Van Johnson smile. "You
should have gotten Sylvester to help you with that bag."

"Your mother couldn't find him," Jeff explained. "It
doesn't matter."

"But that thing looks heavy. Can I help?"

He grinned. "I'm strong. Four years in the Marines
did that much for me, anyway."

I took the master key out of my skirt pocket. "Which

room?" I asked. "At least let me open the door for you."

"Number 14," he said. "I'm moving in. I'm here to stay."

"You mean you're going to live here? You're going to be a regular?" I found myself feeling absurdly pleased with that idea.

"Yes," he said. "This commuting back and forth to New York every day on the Dirty Central is for the birds." He picked up his bag again and started toward Room 14. "I'm going to stay right here as long as this job with Jensen Tool and Die lasts."

I put the key in the lock and turned it. "How long will that be?" I asked.

"I don't know."

I pushed the door open and stood aside as he carried his bag in and set it on the canvas luggage rack. I stood in the doorway and watched as he opened it and began to pile his clothes on one of the beds. "Things are in an awful mess there," he continued. "It'll be a while."

I walked into the room. "Let me help," I said. "I'll hang up the suits while you put the other things away."

"OK," he agreed. "Thanks."

"I thought Mr. Jensen had a good business," I said. "I thought he was very successful and made lots of money. His house in Morristown is almost a mansion."

"You've been there?" Jeff asked, looking up from his pile of socks.

"No," I said, "but my mother has. Mr. Jensen invited her to a party there once."

"His business *is* good," Jeff said. "Very good. But the

books are in a mess. That's what I'm here for. I work for an accounting firm. We do consulting jobs all over the country, setting up proper accounting procedures for companies like Mr. Jensen's—you know, companies that started out small and grew without really noticing. The owner kept all the figures in his head, or else had his Aunt Sadie come in twice a week as a part-time bookkeeper. When you get as big as Jensen Tool & Die is now, you can't operate that way any more."

I patted the sleeve of a soft, cashmere sport coat as I hung it away in the closet. "You don't seem like an accountant," I said.

"And what does an accountant seem like?" he asked. He unloaded half a dozen books from the suitcase and put them on the night table. I glanced at their jackets.

"I never expected an accountant to carry around the Rockwell Kent edition of Shakespeare," I said. "I guess I'm as full of stereotypes as the Civic League ladies."

"Another stereotype," he countered. "They'll get you nowhere." He picked the Shakespeare up and fondled it affectionately. "It's a marvelous one-volume edition," he said. "Would you like to borrow it?"

"Thanks," I said, "but I have it. My mother gave it to me for my birthday." I selected another book from the pile, *The Naked and the Dead* by Norman Mailer. "I'll take this one, though."

He grabbed it out of my hands. "You can't have it," he said. "I'm in the middle of it." Then he grinned apologetically. "Of course you can borrow it when I'm done. It's just that I get kind of tense about books I'm in the middle of. If I misplace them around the house or leave them in the office overnight, or something like that, I go crazy."

"I understand perfectly. I'm the same way." Miss Newcastle, the librarian at the public library, had told me I was too young for *The Naked and the Dead* when I tried to put my name on the reserve list for it. Though in general I was fond enough of Miss Newcastle, I had been furious. If my mother didn't censor my reading, what made her think she had the right to do it? I was afraid Jeff had grabbed the book from my hand for much the same reason. Apparently, I had been wrong. As a human being he put me in the same class as himself. I found that exhilarating.

Suddenly, Dan appeared in the doorway. "Hey, Rachel," he said, "I've been looking all over for you."

"Dan," I said brightly, "do you know Jeff Dulac? Jeff, my brother Dan."

"Hi, Dan," Jeff said. He crossed the room and held out his hand.

Dan looked at Jeff's hand as if it were a dead rodent, then took it gingerly and sort of grunted. He dropped it as quickly as he could and turned to me. "It's impossible to find anyone in this place," he complained. "Mom sent me to look for you. She said for you to get your dinner before the kitchen closes. It's seven-thirty." On weekdays, if there were no parties, the kitchen closed at eight.

"Really?" I was surprised. It was unlike me to let a meal hour slip by unnoticed. "I'm not really hungry. I think I'll just have a salad."

Jeff had returned to his unpacking. "Thanks a million for your help, Rachel," he said. "I really appreciate it."

"So long, Jeff. See you around." I walked out of the room and closed the door behind me. Then I picked up my feet and began to run down the hall.

"Cripes, Rachel," Dan called after me, "what's gotten into you?"

I didn't answer him. I dashed all the way to the end of the hall and down the long flight of steps to the lobby, just the way I used to do when I was little. I didn't feel nearly so miserable about getting my finger stuck in a Coke bottle as I had a couple of hours before. "So there," I told Sir Baldwin, as I passed him on my way into the Holiday Room. "Phooey on you."

V

I sat at one of the little blue-topped tables in a dimly lit corner of the bar. Just as we had a family table in the Holiday Room, where we took our meals and the help took theirs, so we had a family table in the bar, where Mother sat talking with customers like Mr. Jensen on long, quiet evenings. Mother would drink coffee and knit argyle socks. The customers would drink whiskey or beer and smoke cigarettes. Sometimes they'd eat at that table, too, though we rarely did. Mother didn't care for us to hang around the bar. When we asked her why, she just said it didn't look nice, when customers were there.

But there was a show on TV I was bound and determined to see, and the only TV set in the Inn was in back of the bar. The show was a special—Toscanini conducting the NBC Symphony Orchestra. The bar customers wouldn't be much interested in it, I knew. They'd talk through the whole thing. But, if I concentrated on the music, I'd hear it well enough and, if I watched Toscanini's face, I'd understand it. I knew that from the last time I'd watched him conduct. So I was sitting there, reading and sipping a Coke, while I waited for the program to begin.

"Hey, Rachel, you're going to go blind, reading in that light."

I looked up. It was Jeff. "What're you reading anyway?" he asked.

"*Hard Times,*" I said. "It's by Dickens."

"Yeah, I know," he said. "One of his best. It's not so . . . well, not so spread out as some of his others, if you know what I mean."

I knew exactly what he meant. As I had before, I felt a flicker of amazement at an accountant who knew about literature. After all, I knew nothing about accounting. But this time I had enough sense not to express my surprise. I simply nodded my agreement with his remark about *Hard Times.*

"The only other Dickens novels I've read that can compare with it are *A Tale of Two Cities* and *Great Expectations,*" I said. "In the others, the ends have nothing to do with the beginnings. Not that I care. I mean, you're nuts if you read *David Copperfield* for the plot."

Jeff laughed and sat down next to me in the booth. "Boy," he said, "since I came here to live, I've sure done a lot of reading. The whole *New York Times* every day and *The Naked and the Dead,* which is over seven hundred pages long. You can borrow it now, if you still want it."

"Was it good?" I asked. "I don't read a lot of current stuff. I'm still too busy trying to get through the nineteenth century. I won't bother with it if you say not to."

His face grew thoughtful. "It was good. Or, anyway, true. But very raw. I don't know. Maybe you should wait until you're a little older."

"Don't be ridiculous," I said. "Age has nothing to do with anything. I read *Forever Amber* when I was twelve. It didn't hurt me. You really can't learn much from a book, you know. When you're young, you just don't understand those parts."

"Oh," Jeff said, nodding wisely, "and now that you're so old, you understand them all perfectly."

"Of course," I said sweetly. "Don't I look like a woman of the world? A somewhat overweight woman of the world," I added. I didn't want him to think I took myself seriously.

"Are you overweight?" Jeff asked. "I hadn't noticed."

This time I laughed out loud. "Jeff, that's one of the nicest things anyone's ever said to me. I think you need glasses, but don't get them."

"Listen, Rachel," he asked, "how old are you, exactly? I've been here on and off for nearly two weeks, and I still can't figure that out. Sometimes I see you behind that registration desk or helping your mother in the dining room and I think you're twenty-five. Other times you're off to school with Rosie in a plaid skirt and bobby socks and I think you're the same age she is."

"I'm sixteen," I said. "How old are you?"

"Twenty-seven," he replied. "Exactly eleven years older than you."

"Yes," I said, "but that won't last long. When you're thirty-one, I'll be twenty. I'll be starting to catch up."

"Why should you want to?" Jeff asked. If Jeff had been confused about my age, I'd been just as confused about his. When I first met him, I took him for about twenty but, when he wasn't smiling, like now, he looked every bit of the twenty-seven years he claimed.

"There's one thing I can't understand," I said to him. "Why does everyone think it's so wonderful to be young? It's ghastly; I hate it. Only one thing matters—how you look. And I don't look good. I can't wait until I'm in college or something, when maybe some other part of me besides my face and figure will count."

"Rachel," Jeff responded, with an emphatic nod of his head, "I know what you mean."

"Oh, no, you don't," I told him. "You're a man."

"Listen, I didn't reach my full growth until I was twenty-two. Talk about late bloomers—I was the champion. What can a ninety-seven pound weakling do in high school?"

"The same as a hundred and forty-five pound slob does, I guess. Read Dickens. And listen to Toscanini. Well," I added defiantly, "I don't care. Dickens and Toscanini are better company than some stupid boy with pimples and peach fuzz on his face."

Jeff ignored my defiance, no doubt recognizing it for the poor, dishonest thing it was. Not that I wanted to give up Dickens and Toscanini. I wanted them and Billy Colbert, too. "If you're going to listen to the concert," Jeff said, "I'll sit here and listen to it with you, if you don't mind."

"Oh, I don't mind," I said. "I'd love company." He settled himself closer to me, even though there was plenty of room in the booth. I began to chatter. "Do you want something to drink? I'll go to the bar and get it for you, if it isn't anything alcoholic. I can't serve liquor until I'm twenty-one. If it's beer or a highball you want, I can tell Tex, and he'll bring it over. He can just put it on your . . ."

"Shut up, Rachel," Jeff whispered, right in my ear. "The music's beginning." So I shut up. Between that moment and the first intermission, Jeff said only one thing. He said, "At your height, one hundred and forty-five pounds is no more than fifteen pounds over-weight. What's the big deal?" When I tried to reply, he shushed me again. A few minutes later, my mother came in and sat down with us to listen to the music, too.

At intermission, one of the men at the bar said in a loud voice, "Enough of that garbage, bartender. Switch the channel to the cowboy flick."

Tex looked at my mother for a signal. "You're not going to let him change the channel, are you, Mother?" I begged.

Mother shrugged. "What can I do?" she whispered. "He's a customer."

"Hey," Jeff cried, as if he'd just discovered something, "I'm a customer, too!" He got up from his seat and walked over to the bar. "Tex, give me a beer," he said, "and leave the concert on. I'm watching it."

"No one else is," said the stranger with the loud voice.

"No one else wants to watch the cowboy flick either," Jeff said. He was right. It was early and the only other

people at the bar were two couples. They were interested in each other, not the television set.

"Who wins, Mrs. Gold?" Tex called out.

"I guess Jeff does," my mother said, turning on all
her charm for the man who liked Hopalong Cassidy.
"You don't mind terribly, do you?"

He ignored her. "Hey," he yelled angrily at Tex,
"who's she? Why does she get to decide?"

"She owns the place," Tex said, in a stage whisper.
"That's why she gets to decide."

"Oh." The man calmed down suddenly. He finished
his drink in a gulp and then left very quickly.

"No tip," Tex said.

"Another customer down the drain," Mother noted.

"So what?" Tex responded. "He was only passing
through. We'd never have seen him again anyway."

"Whereas I," Jeff announced, "am likely to be here
for the rest of my life."

"Ah—you people say that all the time," Mother
teased him gently. "You never mean it."

"I'm getting very comfortable here," Jeff said. "The
day I decided not to commute back and forth to the
city ten times a week was the smartest day of my life so
far. I've got everything here. Good food, good company,
even music on the TV set. It sure beats an empty apartment."

"You're not married, Jeff?" my mother queried. She
could ask anyone anything. Not me. I could never have
asked Jeff if he were married, though I was dying to
know.

"I was, once," Jeff said. "One of those wartime things. When I got back, well, it just didn't work out. We were strangers." He sighed.

"Any kids?" Mother asked.

Jeff shook his head.

"Well, then," Mother said, "no harm done."

"Except maybe to her and me," Jeff commented, with a touch of bitterness in his voice. For all her charm and shrewdness, there were times when it seemed to me that my mother was remarkably insensitive.

"You must have a girl friend," Mother said.

"I've got lots of girl friends," Jeff replied.

"That means you don't have *a* girl friend," Mother commented.

She was making me nervous. "Aren't you getting kind of personal, Mother?" I interrupted.

"It's OK," Jeff assured me. "I don't mind." Then he turned back to my mother. "Once burned, twice shy," he said. "How about you, Bea? Where's your boy-friend?"

"Oh, come on, Jeff," Mother laughed. "Who'd be interested in me? A widow with three kids to support, and Jewish to boot. In a small town like Waterbridge, single men of sufficient years and broad-mindedness to suit my needs are scarce as hen's teeth."

Jeff looked at her speculatively. "That may be," he said. "But you're a young woman, Bea. You don't look like you were cut out for celibacy."

"No more than you, Jeff, no more than you," my mother responded, with a pat on his hand.

"There are those who are interested, Bea," Jeff

continued softly. "I'm sure of that. I think I'm fairly well-acquainted with one of them."

"Everyone knows Mr. Jensen likes Mother," I interrupted testily. "Much good may it do him."

Jeff turned and stared at me. "Why, Rachel Gold," he said, "what's the matter with you? You couldn't ask for a finer man than Ted Jensen. I do believe you're jealous!"

I decided it would be better not to take such a remark seriously, though I was beginning to know myself well enough to know that it was at least partly true. "Why, Jeff Dulac," I snapped back, "I do believe you're crazy! Now *you* shut up and listen to the music."

Which we did for another half an hour. At least Jeff and I did. Mother had to go talk to some people about a wedding reception. "Listen," I whispered to Jeff, after Mother had left, "I know Mr. Jensen's a nice man. But he's married."

"She's gone," Jeff whispered back. "He hadn't slept with her in the last five years anyway."

"Oh, for God's sake, Jeff, how can you know something like that?"

But he wouldn't answer me. With a smug smile on his face, he returned all of his attention to the music. We sat silently but companionably through the last movement of Beethoven's Sixth Symphony. When it was over, I stood up. It was Saturday night and I was working in the checkroom. I still hadn't set it up. "Thank you, Rachel," Jeff said. "Thank you for a delightful hour."

I looked into his eyes for a second before I replied.

73

He was smiling, but he wasn't teasing me. "I think maybe you ought to thank Toscanini," I replied.

"Him, too," Jeff agreed.

"Well, then, you're welcome." Jeff, too, got up from his seat. "Where're you going?" I asked. "Do you have a date?"

He nodded. "Luckily the concert was early. Otherwise I'd have missed it."

"Maybe you could have listened to it with her."

"No," he replied, with a lift of his eyebrows. "I don't think so."

We walked out into the lobby together. "Who is she?" I asked.

"Oh, just a girl from the office," he replied.

"Is she pretty?"

"Of course she's pretty. I wouldn't go out with a girl who wasn't pretty."

"What does she look like?"

"Rather like your mother, actually. Your mother twenty years ago."

"Humph," I grunted. I couldn't think of anything else to say. He followed me into the cloakroom where he'd left his coat while listening to the concert. I took it off the hanger and handed it to him.

"Well," he said, "good night, Rachel."

"Good night," I mumbled. I turned away from him and began busily to arrange the hangers on the racks in proper numerical order. I made so much noise clacking them together, I didn't even hear him go.

VI

Human beings were packed into the Waterbridge Inn like sardines in a can the Saturday night after Thanksgiving. Mother could really have used my help, but she never said a word about it. As a matter of fact, she found the time to run upstairs just as I had finished dressing and check me over.

"You look perfect, Rachel," she said, kissing my cheek very gently so as not to spoil my makeup. "Absolutely perfect."

"Naturally you think so," I said. "You're my mother."

She turned to Rosie, who had come in to perform such small services as zipping up the back of my dress and handing me the lipstick and eye shadow as I called for them. "Doesn't she look perfect?" she asked Rosie.

"Oh, yes," Rosie agreed. "I never saw her look so good."

"You never saw me look so good," I murmured. "Well, that's not saying much. Rosie, you know you have no taste." But I didn't mean that. Actually, I agreed with them. I felt good—I felt *thin*—in that black dress. My hair, which was thick and very dark, was cut in bangs and turned under at my shoulders. I thought I looked rather like Cleopatra. Maybe all was not lost so far as Billy Colbert was concerned. If he was permanently enamored of pint-sized blonde cheerleaders like Tess and Missy, there was no hope for me. But I thought that, if on this particular night he cast his eye in another direction, I might have as good a chance as anyone. Sally didn't know Missy so she probably hadn't even invited her.

Because she was so busy, Mother had asked Jeff to drive me to the party. He was going out anyway; he had another date with the girl who worked in the office at Jensen Tool and Die, the one he'd gone out with the night of the Toscanini concert. She lived in downtown Waterbridge, so he didn't have to go out of his way to take me to Sally's house.

I met him down in the lobby. "What I can see of you sure looks good," he said, "but then it always does." I wasn't troubled with acne, like a lot of kids my age. At least I'd been spared that. I guess that's what Jeff meant. "Take off your coat," he added. "Let's see the rest of you."

I unbuttoned my coat and made a little curtsy as I held it out with both hands. He uttered a long, low wolf whistle, which embarrassed me terribly. "Don't be absurd, Jeff," I said sharply, and hurried to pull the coat close around my body.

We went outside into the parking lot next to the building and got into the car Jeff had borrowed from Mr. Jensen. Unlike my mother's, it did not date from before the war. It was a brand new Packard and it looked about a hundred feet long. Sally's house was a half-hour walk or a fifteen-minute bike ride from the Inn, but, in the car, unfortunately, it took only two minutes to get there. I enjoyed the car, but that wasn't the main reason I was sorry the ride was so short. I had been looking forward to this party; once I'd gotten the dress I could hardly wait for the day to come. But now that it was here, I suspected that, as happened so often, anticipation might prove superior to the event.

When we pulled up to the curb in front of Sally's big, old, white clapboard house, Jeff turned off the ignition. I think he planned to escort me up the walk and to the front door. I didn't give him the opportunity. "Thanks," I said quickly, and jumped out of the car. I ran up the walk and onto the brightly lit porch. I rang the doorbell. Jeff's car was still parked at the curb. He was waiting to see if I got in all right. The door opened, I waved to him briefly, and went in.

The maid in a gray uniform and a white apron who had opened the door took my coat. I had never seen her when I had come to this house years before to play or for a birthday party. They must have hired her especially for the occasion. It was a fancy party. I glanced at myself in the mirror. I was glad about what I was wearing. It was dressy enough. That glimpse of myself in the mirror turned out to be the best moment of the entire evening.

I went into the big front parlor and stood by the entryway, looking over the room. The doors leading to the back parlor had been pushed open. The two rooms were like one, and they were full of people. I didn't seem to know any of them. I hadn't discussed the party with anyone at school, and no one had discussed it with me. It was a difficult thing to talk about because there was no way of knowing whom Sally had invited, so it had seemed best not to talk about it at all.

Making her way toward me across the crowded room was Sally's mother. A slender, fine-featured woman with curly light brown hair and faded blue eyes, she had once been a rare beauty, if the portrait above the mantel was to be believed. I don't suppose Mrs. Stewart's picture was worth five thousand dollars, but I preferred it infinitely to Sir Baldwin's.

Mrs. Stewart was still very pretty. The story was that, when she was in high school, she had had a hot romance with Myron Braunstein, which was effectively killed through the intervention of both their families. Of course, it was only a story, but in Waterbridge most such stories were at least partly true. Myron Braunstein became Michael Brown and went on to fame and fortune in the foreign service. He was now an assistant secretary of state married to a department store heiress. He and the well-known baritone Todd DeVries, son of the black Baptist minister, were the only famous people Waterbridge had ever produced. I had always gotten a good laugh out of that.

Anyway, Sally's mother had married Craig Stewart, whose family was not quite as old, old Waterbridge as the Vincoops, but was respectable enough. Mr. Stewart worked for the Jersey Central Railroad. He never could have afforded the big Victorian house with its cupola on the roof and its huge magnolia tree in the walled garden. Mrs. Stewart had inherited it from her grandmother, old lady Vincoop.

Mrs. Stewart had always been very, very nice to me, and, from the smile of greeting on her face as she came toward me, I could see her feelings about me had not changed.

"Rachel," she said, taking both my hands into hers, "it's so good to see you, wonderful to see you. I'm so glad you could come. How's your mother? I haven't run into her around town in such a long time."

"Oh, she's fine, Mrs. Stewart," I replied. "She's so busy at the Inn this time of year she doesn't get out much."

"Of course. Your mother is a remarkable woman. An example to all of us."

"Yes. Everyone says so."

"In a way, I envy her. You do look a bit like her, you know." I didn't, but perhaps we shared some expressions, some gestures, some attitudes, because people were always claiming to see a resemblance. "You look marvelous," Mrs. Stewart went on. "You've grown up beautifully, just beautifully. And, I always say, who should wear black? Not old people like us, who look dreadfully washed out in it. Young people, like you, you're the ones who should wear it." I knew then that my dress was absolutely wrong. It was ironic that she, who wanted to let me know that I was not to mind its wrongness, was the one who had let me know that it *was* wrong. If she had said nothing, I might never have guessed.

Not likely, though. I was neither blind nor stupid. I looked around the room and saw all the other girls in neat wool dresses, tweeds and plaids, and one or two velvets, with high necks and long sleeves and pearls around their necks. That's what they were wearing, in spite of the maid in the hall. Then I knew what I was dressed for. I was dressed for a cocktail buffet at the Waterbridge Inn. I was dressed the way women would be who would attend Christmas parties at the Inn in the next few weeks. With my bare shoulders and the startling blackness of the dress against my white skin, I was totally out of place. The tone of the invitation should have given me the clue. Sally had written, "Won't you join us at home for a little celebration opening the holiday season Saturday, November 27, at 8:00 p.m.?" How could I have been so gauche?

One of the wool dresses was coming toward us. It was Sally herself, perfectly recognizable yet totally different from my friend of three years ago. She smiled at me, and her greeting was friendly, but far less effusive than her mother's. An unpleasant notion trotted unbidden across my brain. Had it been her mother's idea to invite me? "Hi, Rachel," she said. "I'm glad you could come."

"Thanks for asking me, Sally. It's nice to see you again." I hadn't even seen her in the summers. She always spent them on Martha's Vineyard.

"Yeah. Same here," Sally said. "Come on over and meet some of the kids from my school."

I followed her into the back parlor. A group was clustered in the bow window, talking to two or three

80

others who were sitting on the window seat. Sally said their names so quickly I didn't catch even one of them, and then she disappeared into the hall to greet some new arrivals.

"Hey, Mary," a tall boy in a red tie said, poking the shoulder of the girl seated next to him, "did you hear how we fixed old Garretson the day before we left?"

The girl called Mary giggled. "I heard," she said.

But he launched into the story anyway, and the others stood around, laughing and interrupting with remarks that might as well have been made in Greek for all I understood them. I drifted out into the hall and then into the dining room, where punch and little sandwiches were laid out on the table. When all else failed, I could always eat.

There in the dining room I found them—the kids from Waterbridge High, standing in an uncomfortable little knot. They must have been the ones Sally had gone to greet a few moments before.

Tess saw me first. She waved her hand eagerly as soon as she caught my eye. "We're over here, Rachel," she called, "over here." As if I could miss them. They were the only people in the room.

Billy Colbert was there, and Carl Hessle, and Cathy and Corrie Crispin and a couple of others. We'd all been in the same class in elementary school from the time I came to Waterbridge in the third grade right through eighth. In those days they grouped us by ability, so before she went to boarding school Sally had been in that class, too.

"I love your dress," Tess said. "I mean, it's simply stunning. So sophisticated." Tess herself was dressed in a cashmere skirt and sweater. Was she just trying to be nice, or did she really not know my dress was all wrong?

"Thanks," I replied shortly. "You look good, too."

"Quite a party," Cathy said. "They even have a maid."

"They always had a maid," Corrie said. "Every time we came here when we were little there was a maid."

"Not a maid," Cathy said. "A cleaning lady. That's different. A cleaning lady doesn't wear a uniform."

"Even my mother has a cleaning lady," said Tina Stadtmueller.

"You think there's going to be dancing or something," Billy asked, "or are we just going to stand around here like lumps all night?"

"Try some punch, Billy," I suggested. "Maybe it's spiked."

"Fat chance," Carl muttered gloomily. Then he brightened up. "I have a bottle in the car, though. I could go get it and pour some in."

"Oh, what a marvelous idea," Tess said. "Go get it. I'll come with you. I can smuggle it in under my sweater. No one will suspect *me*," she finished with a high, sharp giggle.

Carl put his arm around her shoulders and led Tess out of the room. When had they become a couple? I was always the last to know. "Oh, come on," I said to the others, "let's try the punch as it is." I was working hard to make my voice sound gay. "If it's spiked, OK, and if it isn't, well, it's the Stewarts' house; they're entitled to serve whatever kind of punch they want."

Billy turned to me and grinned. "Do you really think that Tess and Carl are going to come back with a bottle? They'll be out in that car for at least an hour. The booze is just an excuse. Don't worry about it."

Something in his tone annoyed me. "I'm not worried," I said.

"Well, you know Tess," Billy persisted. "She tends to get very . . . well, very chummy with the man of the moment."

Since he'd gone with her himself every now and again, I thought that was a pretty lousy thing to say. I liked what he said next better. "Come on, Rache, let's be brave and try some of the sandwiches, too." He was speaking to me, only to me. He took my hand and led me to the alcove where the table was laid. I should have liked that as well, but I didn't. His hand was damp and clammy in mine. Or did it just seem so when I thought about it later?

Sally came into the room then with some of the boarding school kids I'd been talking to—or rather, listening to—earlier. "So here's where you are!" she cried. "Listen, I don't like my Waterbridge friends and my Penn Manor friends separating into two groups. I mean, the whole point of this party is for all my friends to get to be friends with each other. You've met Rachel. This is Billy, and these are the twins, and this is Tina. . . . Oh, Billy," she changed direction suddenly, "you and Tim have something in common." She gestured toward the tall boy in the red tie. "You're both hot shot basketball players." How did Sally know that about Billy? She must have been getting the Water-bridge *Republican* at school.

Tim and Billy started to talk about basketball. At first I thought maybe Tim was Sally's boyfriend, but then the girl called Mary came up and put her arm possessively through his. He smiled down at her, lit-erally smiled *down*, since he was about twice as tall as she was. His smile said, "Oh, you darling little thing." People like Mary always made me feel my every pound. But I stuck with the group, even though I didn't give a tinker's darn about basketball. Neither did Sally, unless she'd changed totally since I'd last seen her, but she stuck with us, too, ignoring, for the moment any-way, the other kids from both Waterbridge and Penn Manor. We had all commenced that thrusting and par-rying that always goes on when you meet new people. How I hated those games. I wondered if they went on forever. Did you ever grow up enough not to have to jockey for position? Could you ever just say, "Hi, I'm Rachel Gold. I like to read and eat. Who are you?"

Sally's glazed eyes and fixed smile showed she was growing bored with the basketball talk and, though she had begun it, she decided to end it. "Listen, you kids," she said, "come on into the living room. My father's rolled back the rug, and there's going to be dancing. I've got to put some decent records on. Other-wise, we'll be listening to Rudy Vallee all night."

"We're coming, we're coming," Billy said. "Let's go, Rachel." He followed Sally and I followed him into the living room. Tess and Carl had returned from their foray to Carl's car. Tess was sitting on a sofa against

84

the wall, flirting with one of the Penn Manor boys and Carl was standing next to her, glowering.

Sally went over to the record player and put some records on the machine. "Hey, kids," she shouted, "shut up for a minute. Come on, shut up."

The crowd quieted down and turned toward her expectantly. "You, Tony," she said to her brother, who was standing by the door, "check the study and the dining room. Make sure everyone's in here. No stragglers allowed."

"What's going on?" one girl called out.

"Game time," cried a boy's voice. "Can't you tell?"

"Oh, whoopee," the girl screeched. "Pin the tail on the donkey."

Tony led in the few kids who'd remained in the study or the dining room as Sally started to explain what we were to do. "I want my new friends and my old friends to get together," she said, "so we're going to have a shoe dance. All the guys take off one shoe and put it in the middle of the floor. All the girls pick a shoe, find its mate, and dance with the fellow who's wearing it."

Without a second's hesitation, I glanced over at Billy. He was standing next to Sally at the victrola. His saddle shoes were black and white, not brown and white, and very dirty. I memorized the dirt.

There were a lot of groans and comments, and a lot of laughter, too, but finally Sally jollied everyone into doing as she said. The girls all shut their eyes while the fellows took off their shoes and piled them in the middle of the floor. The shut eyes were supposed to prevent us from seeing who took off which shoe but, of course, it was already too late for that.

When Sally told us to open our eyes, she was standing as close to the pile of shoes as she could get. "OK, girls," she shouted, "come and get 'em." We surged forward, but she had a head start. With unerring accuracy, she picked Billy's shoe out of the pile. I was so startled to see her holding it up like a trophy that I fell back for a moment. There were more girls than boys at the party, and in two seconds all the shoes were gone. I didn't have anyone's shoe, let alone Billy's.

Tina and a couple of other girls I didn't know were in the same boat I was. "Better luck next time," Sally called to us, as Tony started the music. "We'll play another game in a few minutes and you'll get your chance." She ran off to look for Billy, making a great show along the way of searching the foot of every other boy in the room for the mate to the shoe she was carrying. She squealed with delighted amazement when she finally got to Billy. Lucky Mary did not have to stoop to such idiocy. She went straight to Tim, dangling his enormous oxford by its laces.

"I'm going to get something to eat," I said to Tina, as the voice of Vaughan Monroe singing "Dance, Ballerina, Dance" filled the living room. I had been in the dining room once already and I still hadn't tasted a morsel. "Want to come?"

"Sure," Tina said. The other unpartnered girls came, too. Mr. and Mrs. Stewart were in the dining room, and we talked to them for a few minutes. The music was so loud from the other room that it was hard to think of what to say.

After we'd consumed a handful of sandwiches, Tina and I drifted back into the living room. Tony had put a Frank Sinatra record on the machine, and someone had turned off the overhead lights. Only a couple of lamps on the corner tables remained lit. Some of the couples from the shoe dance had broken up, and there were knots of people talking in corners or by the windows. But Sally was still dancing with Billy. He was holding her very close to him. They weren't talking, and their eyes were shut. There weren't going to be any more games. There wasn't going to be any changing of partners. That was all over.

I knew what would happen later on. They'd go out on the side porch, where Carl and Tess were this very minute, in spite of the cold, and start necking. Billy's wet mouth would be all over Sally's, and, if she'd let him, he'd put his big, sweaty hands inside her dress. I felt sick at the very idea of it. I hadn't liked it in seventh grade when we played kissing games at parties. What made me think I'd like it any better now? Let Sally have Billy. She was welcome to him. I was going home to Peter Lawford and Edward Fairfax Rochester.

I felt both angry and foolish. I had totally misread the entire situation. My dress was a mistake. Sally was a mistake. Billy was a mistake. The whole evening was a mistake. I certainly wasn't spending the rest of it trying to make conversation with the likes of Tina Stadtmueller. Enough was enough.

I went into the hall and used the telephone on the little table under the mirror. I called the Inn. My mother answered. Her voice sounded terribly harried. "Mother," I said, suddenly hesitant, "do you think . . . I know you're frantically busy, but do you think you could come for me?" I could hear the voices and music in the background. I could almost smell the smoke and the beer and the French fried potatoes and the garlic toast. Suddenly I wanted to be there so badly that I stopped apologizing and said simply, "Please, Mother, please come for me. Please."

"I'll be right there," Mother said, without another word. "Wait for me outside."

I went into the kitchen and found the maid. I asked her for my coat and she sent me up into Sally's bedroom to get it. I knew where Sally's bedroom was. I had always envied her that bedroom with its window seat looking out on the magnolia tree. I got my coat and went back downstairs. I peeked into the dining room. Mr. and Mrs. Stewart were still there.

"Good night," I said. "Thanks for having me."

"Going already?" Mrs. Stewart asked. "It's still so early."

"Oh, I must go," I replied airily. "Big day tomorrow . . ." I didn't explain. How could I? I didn't know what I meant myself. "But thanks so much. Merry Christmas and happy New Year."

"Well, to you, too," Mrs. Stewart called after me. But I was already almost out the door. I didn't bother saying good-bye to Sally.

The night was damp and cold and starless, but the air felt good after the stuffy heat inside the house. My mother came before I even began to feel the chill. That was unusual. When she had to pick us up from piano lessons or something like that, she was always late. The phone always rang or someone came in to book a party or the dishwasher broke just as she was about to leave. It was almost impossible for her to get out of the Inn when she said she was going to. But this time she had.

I opened the door and got in. "Thanks," was all I said.

She turned her head toward me. She couldn't see much in the dark. "Why did you want to come home so early?" she asked.

"My dress was all wrong," I said. "Everyone else had on wool, with long sleeves."

"I thought maybe it was too old for you," Mother said, "but you look so good in it."

"Not good enough," I commented bitterly.

"Anything else?" Mother asked. "Besides the dress?"

"God, Mother, isn't it enough to be fat and ugly?" I lashed out. "Isn't that enough?"

"You're not ugly," Mother replied coolly. "I don't think you're fat either but, if you think you are, lose some weight."

"Why should I bother?" I asked. "There isn't a boy in the world who would give me a second glance. It's no help being good at schoolwork either."

"That'll change some day," Mother said confidently. "Believe me, it'll change. You just have to be patient."

"Oh, God, Mother," I cried, "what do you know about it?"

"More than you think," she replied quietly. "Listen to me. If you're ever in real trouble, I'll understand and I'll help. But I'm too busy to listen to self-pity. Being a teen-ager hurts, that's all. But it's a curable disease. Everyone grows out of it."

I sighed. What was the use of continuing the conversation? She knew everything. For the rest of the brief ride I kept quiet. She chattered on about the Inn. "I'm a genius," she said. "I got three hundred people into two rooms that were meant to hold two hundred and fifty. And they're happy. Deep down, people are really sardines. They love being squeezed together."

"Do you need me?" I asked glumly. "I can help now." It might prove a distraction.

"Thanks," she replied, "but we're really done. Everyone's had dinner. I knew you were going out tonight, so I hired Aggie Clem for the cloakroom."

When we entered the lobby, I could see that it really must have been difficult for her to tear herself away to pick me up. All the chairs and sofas were occupied by people escaping the noise, heat, and smoke of the dining rooms or the bar. But not all the faces in the lobby were those of strangers. Mr. Jensen and Major Dunleigh were seated in two wing chairs opposite each other, smoking and talking.

I turned to my mother. "What's he doing here?" I asked.

"The bar's so crowded, Major Dunleigh's usual table

was occupied before he came down," Mother explained.

Mrs. Dunleigh went to sleep early, and the Major spent many evenings sitting in the bar, sipping bourbon and soda. But I wasn't talking about the Major. "I mean Mr. Jensen," I said. "He can't be working late on a Saturday night, and it's way past dinner time."

"Don't worry, Rachel," Mother said quickly, "he's not sleeping in your room, though we're full. He's sleeping with Jeff."

"But what's he doing here?" I persisted. "What's he doing here on a Saturday night?"

Mother eyed me narrowly. "I guess he didn't have anything better to do," she said. "This is a public place."

He had seen us. He got up and crossed the lobby. "Where'd you disappear to, Bea?" he asked. "I was looking all over for you." He smiled at her, not just with his mouth, but with his eyes, too.

"Rachel called," Mother told him. "I went to get her."

"You should have asked me," Mr. Jensen replied. "I'd have gone. You're so busy." He moved behind her and put his hands on her shoulders. "Let me take your coat. You look so tired."

"I am tired," she replied. "But in another couple of hours it'll all be over. I'll be able to soak in a hot tub for as long as I want." She slipped her arms out of her coat, stretching her shoulders as she did so. "If only I had a foot massager. I always meant to tell the kids to get me one of those things for my birthday."

91

"I'm a superior foot massager," Mr. Jensen said. "Later, I'll show you my license." He laughed, and his eyes glinted. I looked from them up into the eyes of the portrait, into Sir Baldwin's eyes. Baldy wasn't smiling, but it seemed to me that the glint in his eyes was the same as the glint in Mr. Jensen's. Mr. Jensen was generous and good-natured. Sir Baldwin was cruel and arrogant. But the glint in their eyes was the same. "Be careful," I said suddenly to Mr. Jensen. "Be careful or Baldy will get you."

The glint faded and was replaced by a look of concern. "Baldy?" Mr. Jensen asked.

"Sir Baldwin MacClough," I said. "The man in the painting."

"But why would he want to get me?" Mr. Jensen asked, humoring me.

"Mother's in love with him," I said. "He looks to me to be a jealous type."

"But who does Sir Baldwin love?" Mr. Jensen retorted. "That's the question. Maybe you!"

"Don't be ridiculous," I responded, feeling anger rise up into my throat. "He hates me." I turned away from them and walked toward the steps as quickly as I could without actually running. They must have thought I was crazy, both of them, but I didn't care.

When I got upstairs, I undressed and got into bed. I read a Georgette Heyer novel I'd just picked up in the library. She was an unfailing comfort.

After a while, I put out the light. I could hear, coming up through the floor, the thump, thump, thump of the Hammond organ in the bar directly below my bedroom. Not the melody, only the thump, thump, thump of the rhythm. It was a familiar, comforting sound. I had fallen asleep to it countless times, and that night, even that awful night, that thump, thump, thump sent me to sleep once again.

VII

Late afternoon was Mother's relaxing time. She soaked in the tub for perhaps half an hour before getting dressed for the evening. Rosie and I could talk to her then; it was really our only opportunity. I don't know when Dan talked to her. Maybe never. It was hard to know whether that was due to choice or circumstance. Yet I think she loved Dan best. No, that isn't true. She didn't love him better than she loved Rosie or me. She just worried about him more.

I sat on the toilet while Mother lay back in the tub, head and feet the only parts of her not submerged. But I could see her whole body, her breasts, her stomach, her legs, shimmering palely in the green water.

"Captain Kreiss just called," I told her. "He said to tell you he won't be by tonight after all."

"Thank goodness," Mother murmured.

"Why?" I asked. "I thought you liked Captain Kreiss. Remember the time you asked us if we thought you should marry him?"

She nodded. "But Rosie was right when she said he's for fun, not for father. I was just talking. I didn't really

94

mean to marry him. Or perhaps I ought to put it the other way around. He didn't really mean to marry me." She began rubbing her legs with a bar of soap. "He's just not a family man."

Captain Kreiss had been Mother's boyfriend during the war. He'd been stationed at a supply depot outside of Waterbridge. Of course, he was plain Dr. Kreiss now, but we still called him Captain Kreiss. We had only seen him a few times since the war had ended. He had called early that day and said he'd be spending the night at the Inn on his way to a medical convention in Philadelphia. But then he called back later to say there'd been an emergency and he wasn't coming after all. "I thought you'd be disappointed at not seeing him again," I told my mother.

"Well, you know," Mother said, "Ted will be here tonight." Ted. That was Mr. Jensen. "I dreaded having two men on my hands at once. That may be all right at your age but, when you're as old as I am, you won't enjoy it. It's too exhausting."

I'd have been happy to have just one man, any man, show some real interest in me, whether I returned that interest or not. What right had she to complain about two? But I didn't say that.

Instead I said, suddenly bold, "Mother, I want to ask you a question."

"What?" She took the washcloth off the side of the tub and scrubbed her face.

"Do you think it's all right to make love if you're not married? You know—go all the way. Have intercourse." The articles and stories in *The Ladies Home Journal* were perfectly clear on the subject. It was not all right. But I'd read enough and even seen enough to know there had to be other opinions.

However, the question I was asking was not the question I really wanted to ask. What I really wanted to ask was whether or not she and Captain Kreiss had made love, or she and Mr. Jensen. But that bold I wasn't. Besides, maybe I didn't want to know the answer to that question—not really.

Mother put the washcloth back on the side of the tub and smoothed it out carefully. "Once you start in with sex," she replied slowly, "it's hard to stop. It gets to be something you find it difficult to do without."

"It's that good, huh?" Perhaps once they got past their eighteenth year, boys' hands and mouths no longer felt so damp.

"Well," she continued, choosing her words with care, "not necessarily at first. You see, I think you need a lover you're really fond of, and one who's very fond of you. Because, well . . . in the beginning it takes a certain amount of patience. But then, once you know what you're doing, it's wonderful. Really, it's the best thing in the world. So you don't want to give it up. That's why I think it's best to wait until you're married to get started."

"But you don't think God will strike you dead if you're not a virgin on your wedding day? If there is a God."

"My Cousin Fagie thought God would strike her dead if she put a piece of bacon in her mouth," Mother said. "She did and He didn't. God, I hope, has more

96

important things to worry about. But I don't think a woman can sleep with a man without getting emotionally involved, and that's why I think she's better off waiting until she's married. It's just safer, that's all."

I nodded. It all sounded very sensible. I knew there weren't five girls at Waterbridge High School in the year 1948 who could have asked their mothers that question and gotten a reasonable answer. And what were mothers for if not to answer questions like that? For crocheting antimacassars? After all, I knew perfectly well that one person can't have everything, least of all in a mother.

Except, of course, for Sir Baldy. He'd had everything, and had thought it was coming to him. As I passed his portrait on my way into the Holiday Room for dinner, I paused and looked at him. I still hated him, but I was getting kind of used to him. "You wanted something, you just grabbed it, didn't you?" I said to him silently. " 'Droit de seigneur' and all that. Well, some people might admire that kind of behavior, but I don't. I don't and I never will."

He didn't say anything. He just went right on sneering, and I went right on into the Holiday Room.

Dan and Rosie were already seated at our table, eating roast chicken and listening to their serials on the radio. I pushed through the swinging doors into the kitchen and asked Luke for some chicken for myself. I stood chatting with him while he dished it up, and then I carried my plate back into the Holiday Room. As I put it down on the table, Mother came in, dressed now for the evening, though the fine tendrils of her hair still

97

curled damply from her bath. "It's slow tonight," she announced. "I think I'll have dinner with you."

"What do you want?" I asked. "I'll order it for you." She ate with us so seldom I felt as if I were a hostess and she my guest.

"That's all right," she said, sitting down opposite Rosie. "I saw Min in the lobby and I told her what to bring me."

Just then Min came through the swinging doors carrying Mother's appetizer, a half grapefruit topped with a maraschino cherry. She put it down in front of Mother and then went away again. Mother began to eat, glancing around the table at the three of us. "Isn't this nice?" she said. "Except for the radio. Rosie, please turn off that radio."

"Turn it off please, Dan," Rosie passed on the request. To my surprise, Dan did not say, "She asked you. You do it." He obeyed Rosie. My mother shot them each a curious glance, but she made no comment. I, too, looked from one to the other. And then, at about the same moment, she and I both noticed that Rosie was behaving rather strangely, sawing away at her chicken, popping one piece into her mouth and then apparently dumping the next piece in her lap.

"Rosie Gold," Mother asked sharply, "what in the name of heaven are you doing?"

Rosie looked up, her blue eyes wide and innocent. "I can't eat all of this meat. Some of it's for Buster."

"Where is Buster?" Mother asked, as if she didn't know.

Rosie's eyes looked away from Mother's. "On my

lap," she admitted, trying to make her reply sound very offhand.

As if on cue, Buster, who had been absolutely silent up until this point, let out a yelp. We knew Rosie had sinned. Buster was not permitted in the bar, the dining rooms, or the kitchen. The Dunleighs had agreed to that condition when they had come. But we couldn't help laughing, all of us at the table except Rosie herself, when Buster let out that yelp. We laughed so loud that the door to the Holiday Room was pushed open and there, in the doorway, stood Jeff and Mr. Jensen.

"Hey, what's the joke?" Jeff asked.

Rosie stood up. "I'm taking Buster to Mrs. Dunleigh," she said righteously. "He's been naughty. Have you had dinner?"

"No," Mr. Jensen said, "as a matter of fact, we haven't."

"Then why don't you join us?" Rosie flashed them her incandescent smile, which was just like Mother's, and then tripped out of the room. That child could wriggle out of anything. I wished I had had half her genius.

Mr. Jensen and Jeff pulled chairs up to the table. The nice thing about a round table is that it can seat an almost infinite number of people, as King Arthur found out long ago.

"Very kind of you to let two lonesome bachelors join you," Mr. Jensen said.

Min came in to bring my mother her lamb chop and salad. She took Jeff's and Mr. Jensen's orders and, before she was done, Rosie had returned to the table, slipping back into her place virtually unnoticed.

Mr. Jensen had seated himself next to my mother, his arm draped casually around the back of her chair as he waited for his food. Jeff had pulled up a chair between Mother and me.

Mother smiled, first at Mr. Jensen and then at Jeff. "I hope you gentlemen had a good day," she said.

"Oh, I did," Jeff replied. "I did." He turned toward me. "Rachel—remember the bookkeeper I told you about?"

"Aunt Sadie," I said.

Jeff laughed. "Only at Jensen Tool and Die her name is Mrs. MacIlheny." Mother wrinkled her brow. She had no idea what we were talking about. "I had a fight with her today you wouldn't believe," Jeff continued. "They could hear us all the way out in the plant. Or they could hear her, anyway. I stayed calm."

"In that Brooks Brothers tie, what else?" I commented.

Jeff laughed again. I hadn't known I was so witty. Then he launched into an elaborate and very funny impression of Mrs. MacIlheny. Mother laughed hugely every time he paused for breath. She could hear him even though most of the time his head was turned toward me.

Dan left the table after eating his ice cream, but the rest of us lingered there over coffee. I stayed longer than I should have, for I had a lot of studying to do. But it was so pleasant at the table. Somehow we got to talking about radio programs and Rosie urged me to do my soap opera, "Elevator," all about these people who'd been stuck on an elevator for seventeen years. It didn't matter when you tuned in, they were still stuck on the elevator. I commonly entertained the family with this saga on summer Sunday nights as we drove home from the beach. Jeff caught on quickly and chimed in, playing all the men's parts. Actually, he was much better at ad libs and imitations than I was.

But then the party broke up. Min came in to tell my mother someone was in the lobby inquiring about a wedding, so she had to leave. Mr. Jensen wasn't far behind her. He was going into the bar to have a beer and watch a little television before he went to bed. "Me, too," Jeff said, as he rose from the table. "You want to come?" he asked me. "Milton Berle isn't ex-actly Toscanini, but he's good for a few laughs."

"I'll come," Rosie said.

"Don't you have homework?" I asked her.

"I did it earlier," she said. "I did it when I first got home from school." I knew she was telling the truth. She was as good a student as I'd been at her age, with half the effort. But I couldn't go into the bar to watch Milton Berle. I had to get my lab report done for the next day, and there was a lot of calculation involved, which always took me hours.

So I went upstairs to do my work. I really didn't mind missing Milton Berle. I couldn't possibly laugh as hard at him as I had at Jeff Dulac's additions to the latest episode of "Elevator." I couldn't remember a pleasanter dinner than the one we had just had.

But I wasn't so happy later, in the middle of the night, when I got up to go to the bathroom. I walked down the chilly hall in my bare feet, my robe clutched about me. I opened the bathroom door, closed it behind me, and locked it. Then I heard voices. Two voices. They were coming from my mother's room. One voice was my mother's, the other was a man's. Not Dan's, but a grown man's. I guessed that answered the question I hadn't had the nerve to ask earlier that afternoon, the one to which I really hadn't wanted to know the answer. I left the bathroom as quickly as I could and went to the public one down the corridor. It seemed better to do that than to sit there, on the toilet, listening to the sound of those two voices.

VIII

Not long after that pleasant dinner we had another party, one that we had every year—the Inn's annual Christmas celebration. As a child, I had always enjoyed it. In those days it had contented me just to be allowed to stay up late, watching the staff metamorphosed by liquor and their best clothes; they were like the cinder maiden turned into a princess in the fairy tale. Santa Claus, in the person of Mother's favorite liquor salesman, Mr. Neumann, thinly disguised by a rented red suit and a pillow tied around his middle, always gave out presents at midnight. After that, we three were sent to bed. Mother didn't want us around when the drinking got serious.

But last year she had let us stay until the end—all of us, including Rosie. The youngest gets to do things sooner than the eldest ever does. And this year she would let us stay until the end again, if we wanted to.

By the time I got down to the bar, almost everyone else was already there. Occupying all the barstools, they were scarcely recognizable in the dim, soft light, and the sounds of their laughter and conversation and the clink of ice in their glasses made me hesitate as I stood in the doorway. What was I doing here, after all? Watching no longer satisfied me. I wanted to dance myself. This year, if I couldn't actually be a part of the party, I wasn't sure I cared to be there at all. Dan wasn't there, at least not yet. Before I'd come down, I'd looked in his room. He had been lying on his back on his bed, his hands under his head, his knees up, still dressed in an old, striped polo shirt and corduroy pants with patched knees. He was listening to the radio. "Aren't you getting dressed?" I'd asked him.

"Nah," he'd replied. "Maybe later, if there's something decent to eat."

"Don't you want to hear the music?"

Dan snorted. "Izzie Spanker and his Merry Music Makers? That's not music. That's warmed-over Guy Lombardo."

I knew that after a while Mother or Luke would come up to get him, so I didn't press. He had enough people worrying about him already.

"How do I look?" I asked him.

He turned over on his side so he could see me better. "Old," he said. "Thinner, too."

I was satisfied. And what finally sent me through the doorway and up to the bar was the feeling that it would be a shame to waste the black dress when I might never have another chance to wear it. For this occasion at least it was absolutely the right thing. Everyone always dressed up fit to kill for the Inn's Christmas party. I was standing next to Min, who was drinking a sickening mixture of gin, cream, grenadine, and apple jack called a pink lady. The neon brightness of Min's drink exactly matched her pink satin sheath with ruffles on the hem and around the low, round neckline. It was so tight across her plump bust and thick hips and thighs that she must have struggled half an hour to get into it. Min loved great big earrings and always wore them, even when she was dressed in her white waitress uniform. Tonight her earrings were huge, pink enameled flowers with rhinestone centers.

"Hullo, Rachel," Min said. "Where you been hiding? You spent so much time dolling yourself up you almost missed the whole party. But it was worth it. You look terrific."

"So do you, Min," I said politely.

"Hey, Tommy," Min called in her booming voice, "fix up my buddy Rachel here."

Tommy, Min's husband, was a skinny, dried-up little man, no taller than she, but about one-eighth her width. I never saw Min without a smile; I never saw Tommy with one. But Tommy, by trade a groundskeeper on a big estate in Far Hills, loved to tend bar, and he did it every year at the Christmas party to give Tex the night off. "What'll it be, Rachel?" Tommy asked me. "Old enough this year for something with a little kick in it? How about a pink lady, like Minnie's?"

The mere sight of that nauseating concoction was enough to turn my stomach. "I think I'll stick to Coke for another year at least," I said.

"Probably a wise decision." Tommy himself was sipping a beer in between mixing drinks for everyone else. He poured a Coke into an ice-filled glass and set it up on the bar for me.

Seated on the other side of me was a woman I didn't know. I didn't think she was more than twenty, and she was wearing what seemed to be a prom dress. It had a strapless shirred blue top and a big, billowing, blue net skirt. She was drinking something quite as horrid-looking as Min's drink, only it was green and called, I believe, a grasshopper. Tex was seated on the other side of her. He called out to me, "Rachel, I'd like you to meet my friend, Sheila. Sheila Bolenkrantz."

"Hi, Sheila," I said. Each year Tex brought a different girl to the party, and each year the girl was younger than the one from the year before. In another year or two, Tex wouldn't have to go looking for someone to bring. He could come with Rosie.

Sheila smiled at me. I guess she was glad to see someone in the room moderately close to her own age. "Hey," she whispered, "you and your date sit at the same table as me and Tex, OK? If you don't, I'll feel like I'm in the middle of a cemetery or something."

"Gee, Sheila," I whispered back, "I'm awfully sorry, but I didn't come with a date."

"You didn't?" Sheila's round blue eyes opened wide. "Who did you come with?"

"My mother," I confided. "I guess I'd better sit with her."

"Rachel's the boss's daughter," Tex explained, just in time. A wary look crossed Sheila's face. "Oh," she said. "Nice to meet you, I'm sure." Then she turned back to Tex. I moved away from the bar, clutching my icy Coke glass in my hand. I glanced over to the booth in the corner where Rosie was sitting. She was with Luke and his wife Maybelle, and their two great big daughters, Nellie and Cleo, and Nellie's husband, Quinn, and Cleo's boyfriend, Crosby. Only someone as short as Rosie could have squeezed herself in among that many broad-shouldered, wide-hipped people. They were all laughing out loud, except for Rosie, who sat in the middle with a pleased little smile on her face. So they were laughing at something Rosie had said. She was still young enough to be cute. Maybe Rosie was the kind of person who would always be cute. Maybe that was another good thing that went with being the youngest.

I glanced up and down the bar. Nearly everyone was there with someone. Even Mother was deep in conversation with Mr. Jensen. This was the first year Mr. Jensen had come, the first year since the days of Captain Kreiss that Mother had had what you could call a date for the party. Besides us kids, the only person who was not half of a couple was Sylvester. He was at the very end of the bar, with a shot glass and a bottle of rye in front of him. He would down straight shots until he fell off the barstool. Someone would then stretch him out on one of the sofas in the lobby, where he would sleep until the party was over. That was Sylvester's idea of a good time. There was no point in going over and talking to Sylvester.

I headed out of the bar in the direction of the kitchen. I would check out the buffet, which was always marvelous for this party. There'd be fried chicken, sliced steak, butterfly macaroni in meat sauce, chow mein, barbecued spare ribs, and big bowls of green salad, potato salad, and cole slaw. For dessert, there'd be a sweet table with a hundred different kinds of cakes and cookies, each one the carefully wrought offering of one of the guests. When there was nothing else to do, I could always eat.

In the empty lobby I stopped for a moment to look at Baldy. "Hey," I asked him silently, "do you want to be my date for the Christmas party? You're entitled to come. You're certainly a regular." Then I felt a breath of cold wind on my back. The front door must have opened. I turned to see who had come into the building. It was Jeff. His face looked like a black cloud, but it brightened when he saw me. "Hey Rachel," he said, "you look great. Absolutely fantastic."

"Oh," I said deprecatingly, "you saw this dress before, the night you drove me to the party."

"Yeah. You looked great that night, too. Did you have a good time?"

"Lousy," I replied briefly.

He raised his eyebrows. "Really? I'm damned sorry to hear that. Listen, let me put my coat away, and then you can tell me all about it, and I can tell you all about how my date stood me up tonight."

"Your date stood you up?" I echoed in amazement. Why would anyone stand Jeff up? Besides bearing a marked resemblance to Van Johnson, he was more fun to talk to than anyone else I knew. Most of the time when you talk to people, nothing happens. It's all just, "Pass me the salt," and "Remember to pick up some shampoo for me when you go to the drugstore." But, when I talked to Jeff, I felt that he was touching my mind and I was touching his. So even if he'd looked like Charles Laughton in *The Hunchback of Notre Dame*, I wouldn't have stood him up. I went with him up the stairs and down the hall to his room, and stood leaning against the door jamb while he hung up his coat. "Who was it?" I asked. "Who stood you up?"

"Oh, I told you about her," Jeff replied. "She's the girl from the office I've been seeing lately."

"You got to her house and she wasn't there?" I asked. I was curious about the whole thing. How did someone go about standing someone else up?

"Her mother said she was in bed with a cold, but I don't believe that," Jeff said. "I spoke to her this afternoon and she was fine. Something better came along, that's all."

"How could anything be better than you?" I asked with a smile, as if I were joking.

Jeff laughed. "Maybe I should have said richer. That's not hard at all."

"Oh, then," I commented, "you know who it is."

"I have a pretty good idea," Jeff said. "But it doesn't matter. Not really. It's a blow to my ego, but that's all. She doesn't matter. She's just a party girl." Suddenly he grinned. "Come on, gorgeous," he said, "you be my date. You're not ashamed to be seen with an old man like me, are you?"

"I don't think of you as an old man," I replied seriously.

He dropped his phony, lighthearted manner and

spoke to me with equal seriousness. "I am though, you know. I'm twenty-seven. I'm exactly eleven years older than you are."

I nodded. He'd told me that before. Then he took my arm and put it through his, smiling once again. "Now you tell me just what happened to you at that party. Why didn't you tell me about it before this?"

"Jeff, I haven't really seen you to talk to you since that night we all had dinner together."

"Yeah, I know," he admitted. "I've been working like crazy, trying to get done. I haven't been home before ten one night this week. But I'm here now, so tell me. What happened?"

"Nothing happened," I replied. "I guess that was the trouble. I had my hopes up too high. There's this boy, Billy, and, well . . . in my new dress I thought maybe he'd see me in a new way, but it turned out the one he saw was Sally, and my dress was all wrong, and, I don't know, it was a mess. I didn't belong there. So now let's forget about it. It doesn't matter." And suddenly it really didn't matter. It didn't matter at all.

By this time we were back downstairs in the bar. Everyone now had had enough to drink and the party was in full swing. The noise was so deafening that it was a good thing the Inn was closed to regular business after nine this one particular evening of the year. Any unsuspecting customer would have had his eardrums shattered.

In a moment Jeff and I were swept up into the talk and smoke and laughter. Jeff drank scotch and I drank

Cokes and we talked with Mother and Mr. Jensen, with Tex and Sheila, and with Mr. and Mrs. Neumann. For a while we squeezed into the booth in which Luke and his family were seated and laughed and joked with them, and then it was time to go in for supper. The food was as good as ever that year, I'm sure, but I didn't eat very much. Jeff and I were too busy dancing. I danced with other people, too—with Pedro, the salad man, and with Tommy, and with Tex. I danced with whoever asked me, even with Sylvester, who collapsed rather later than usual. I didn't much like dancing with him because his breath smelled of rye and his body just smelled, but Mother was watching me and I knew I couldn't say no. The second time he approached us from across the room, however, Jeff saw him. He pulled out my chair before I knew what he was doing, and in an instant we were waltzing across the floor. I didn't know how to waltz, but that didn't seem to matter very much. We didn't sit down after the waltz because the next set was fox trots. Someone had turned out the overhead lights and only the candles on the tables glimmered in the darkened room. Jeff held me very close to him and we moved silently through the dimness. I felt lightheaded, as if I really had been drinking, or as if I were in a smoky golden dream.

When the band took a break, Jeff and I went into the kitchen to get coffee for our table. I was standing at the urn running coffee into a metal pot and Jeff was piling cups and saucers on a tray. When I had filled the pot, he put down the tray and took the pot out of my hands and put that down, too. He placed his hands on my shoulders. "The innkeeper's daughter," he said softly. "The innkeeper's black-eyed daughter."

I was shaking, but I managed a little laugh. "Landlord's daughter," I corrected him.

"What?"

"You're quoting 'The Highwayman,'" I explained. "It's 'Bess, the landlord's daughter, the landlord's black-eyed daughter.'"

"Oh, Rachel," he said, a smiling glint in his eye, "what am I going to do with you? What am I going to do with you?" And then he put his arms all the way around me and pulled me close to him and kissed me. It was a long, warm kiss. I kissed him, too. We stood pressed together, our arms wrapped around each other, our mouths drinking each other in, for a long time. I didn't notice an inappropriate amount of dampness about either Jeff's hands or his lips. I didn't notice much of anything. For once in my life, I was just feeling. But then I stopped kissing him. After all, I hadn't kissed anyone before, except for those games of post office and spin the bottle in sixth and seventh grades. I didn't know what to do about what was going on inside of me.

Jeff sensed that. When I broke away, he let me go. "I think we'd better get this coffee in there," I said, struggling for breath. "If we don't, they'll come after it."

"Yeah," Jeff agreed.

"Wipe off the lipstick," I suggested.

He did so, absently.

We went back into the Holiday Room. Everyone was

eating dessert and drinking coffee, except, of course, the people at our table because we had been so long about bringing it. My mother looked at me for a moment, but she didn't say anything. The band started up again, playing its final set, breaking into "Good Night, Ladies" exactly at two o'clock. We danced the final set, too, Jeff and I. Everyone did, except Sylvester, asleep at last on his couch in the lobby, and Dan and Rosie. I didn't know where they were. I guess they'd gone to bed. I hadn't noticed them for hours.

When the last strains of "Good Night, Ladies" had died, Mother turned up the lights with a sigh of relief. She was always relieved when the party was over, happy to have gotten through it without anyone's getting into a fight, or breaking anything, or getting sick. She stood at the door saying good night and kissing everyone and agreeing that this had been the best party ever. Mr. Jensen, Jeff, and I were sprawled exhausted on chairs in the lobby. I felt suddenly flat and tired, too tired to say anything. Jeff was silent, too. Only Mr. Jensen was able to work up sufficient energy to speak. "Well, Jeff," he said, "this sure was a nice going-away party for you, wasn't it?"

"I didn't think of it that way," Jeff said, with a slight smile, "but I guess it was. I guess it was."

"You're leaving?" I asked. I wasn't surprised. I knew he'd be leaving one of these days. Everyone always did leave the Inn, sooner or later, except us. Even the help. But I hadn't realized it would be so soon.

He looked at me. "Yes," he replied softly. "I've been working late all week so I could finish up at Jensen

Tool and Die before Christmas. I'm going to my parents' for Christmas, and I thought it would be more convenient if I didn't come back afterward. I'll just go right on to the new job."

"Where's that?" I asked. I didn't really care. I cared that he was going, but what did it matter where?

"Toledo," he said. "Toledo, Ohio."

I nodded and pressed my lips tightly together. When I felt that I could speak again, I stood up. "Good night, Jeff," I said. "I'm tired. I think I'll go to bed now."

Jeff stood up. "I'll walk you to your room," he said.

"No, thanks," I replied. How could he admit to his departure so casually? How could he kiss me so warmly one minute and tell me he was going the next, as if it wasn't supposed to matter at all to either of us? Why hadn't he told me himself, warned me somehow? I felt as if I'd suddenly taken a step into midair. The last thing I needed now was more of his kisses up there in the empty hall.

I stood up. "I'll see you in the morning," I said. In the morning when the light is bright enough to chase away any dream shadows that might linger in a foolish brain. "Good night, Mr. Jensen." I hurried away from both of them and up the stairs.

I had barely reached my room and started to undress when there was a knock on my door. Someone had hurried up the steps as fast as I. I hadn't even had a chance to start to cry. I was saving that luxury for when I was in bed.

It wasn't Jeff at my door, though. It was my mother.

She came in and sat down on my bed. I went on undressing.

"It was a nice party, wasn't it?" she said.

"Yes," I agreed. I didn't expand.

"It always is," she said. "But I always worry. I remember that one year when Klaus worked for us . . ."

"That only happened once," I interrupted. "It's been nice every other time."

She nodded her agreement. For a moment she said nothing, and then she spoke again. "It's just as well he's leaving, you know."

"Is it?" I replied shortly.

"You need boys your own age," she said.

"Boys my own age don't seem to need me," I said. "What am I supposed to do about that?"

"They will," Mother said. "I promise you, they will."

I pulled my brush through my hair, hard. "I don't believe you," I said. "I just don't believe you."

"Well, then," my mother answered me quietly, "if you don't believe me, you've missed the whole point of Jeff."

I didn't reply. I just kept brushing my hair. "The whole point of Jeff," she continued, "is that he's a very attractive man, and he likes you very much. He's liked you all along. That was obvious to me. But, until tonight, he kept his distance. It would have been totally irresponsible of him to do otherwise. Tonight, though, he didn't keep his distance, did he? So it's just as well he's going away. But if you can't believe in yourself after tonight, then you're just plain dumb."

"Everyone goes away from here," I said. "Everyone always goes away. Dan's smart. He doesn't bother with them at all. That way he doesn't get hurt."

"Oh, yes," Mother said, getting off the bed and coming toward me. "Dan's very smart." She took the brush out of my hand and began to brush the back of my hair herself. "He buries his feelings a hundred feet deep. Is that a good thing? You hurt, so at least you know you're alive!"

"What will I do now?" I asked. The question sounded odd, even to my own ears.

"Write a poem," Mother said. "People go away from here, but other people come." She kissed me. "Good night, baby," she said.

"Good night, Mother," I replied. "Thanks."

Thanks for what? She couldn't take away the sick feeling of loss that I had in my stomach, or the anger that Jeff had not told me himself that he was leaving. But I had lost things before, like my father, whom I could remember, even if Dan and Rosie could not. Things come and things go. A person has to get used to that.

I cried for a little while, taking a kind of melancholy delight in my own tears, and then I fell asleep.

IX

New Year's Eve day Dan, Rosie, and I spent the afternoon in the Holiday Room blowing up balloons. It was one job even Dan didn't mind because we used an air compressor the painter lent us. We put the balloons over a hole on the compressor and air wooshed right into them. It took hours, though, because Mother needed hundreds of balloons for the New Year's Eve party that night. Dan had brought his radio downstairs and we listened to it while we worked.

It was five o'clock and already dark when Min came in with a couple of banquet girls to set the room up.

"What's it like out, Merle?" Min asked. She was talking to a girl who'd never worked at the Inn before.

"Bitter," Merle replied. "It got awfully cold awfully fast."

"Boy," Min said, "you can bet if I didn't have to work New Year's Eve, I wouldn't be going out. I'd stay right at home with a bottle of gin and a big fire, listening to Guy Lombardo on the radio."

"Yeah," Merle said, "me, too."

"These people are crazy," Min added.

"I think New Year's Eve is fun." Rosie never let a conversation pass. "All these hats and noisemakers." She waved at the cartons filled with all the junk which the waitresses would have to put on the tables. "I think it's fun."

"You wouldn't think it was so much fun, Miss, if you had to work it," Min said sharply. "Amateur night. You spend most of your time trying to calm down the drunks and what do you get for it? Dirty looks, mostly, and half of 'em stiff you."

"Well," Merle said, "it's so cold maybe there won't be much of a crowd. The wind makes it even worse."

Min looked at her in disgust. "That's a dumb thing to say. Don't let Mrs. Gold hear you talking like that."

The waitress looked annoyed. She hadn't expected Min to scold her. "But you . . ."

"I said I didn't like New Year's Eve customers," Min interrupted. "I didn't say I hoped they'd stay away. And don't you say it either!"

"All right, I won't," the waitress replied. "Don't be so touchy." She flounced out through the kitchen doors. "Dumb," Min muttered, loud enough so Merle and I could both hear her.

For a while there was no more talk—only the sounds of our serials on the radio and the rattle of dishes, silver, and glasses as the waitresses set the tables. In the middle of "Captain Midnight," I heard the fire sirens ring out and Rosie said, dreamily, "I always have the funniest feeling when I hear a fire siren. I wonder if

118

it's us that's on fire." I knew what she meant. When I was her age, I had always wondered that, too.

The fire sirens were heard again, their screeches penetrating through the drawn drapes and into the bright, quiet room. I got up and went toward a window. I meant to draw back the drape and look at the fire engines, which sounded as if they were passing on the highway right in front of the Inn.

At that moment, Mother came into the Holiday Room. She was wearing her coat and carrying ours. "Put these on," she said calmly. "You, too," she called to the waitresses. "Get your coats and leave." Her calmness was careful, like something she was working at. "There's a little fire in the attic. It's nothing, but the firemen said we'd better play it safe and vacate the building."

"So it is us," Rosie said very softly. "The sirens we heard were for us."

"Yes," Mother said. "Come on now." The waitresses had already disappeared into the kitchen. Mother hustled the three of us out into the lobby. A fireman was coming down the steps. It was Harry Fust, who was in the maintenance department at Carbon Chemical. He'd had his wedding reception at the Inn just a little over a year before. "What do you think I should take with me?" Mother asked him.

"Now, Mrs. Gold, don't worry," he replied, as if he were speaking to a two-year-old who'd had a nightmare. "We'll have you back in here in no time at all. It's just a little electrical fire in the attic. Too much smoke for me to actually get up there to look. We'll have to reach it from outside. But don't worry. It's not going to kill your New Year's Eve. In half an hour, it'll all be over."

Mother wanted to grab her cashbox and her green date book from her office, but Harry Fust wouldn't let her. He made us wait outside while he went to get them. The four of us stood in the parking lot. It was bitterly cold, with a wild, biting wind snapping at our cheeks and fingers. There were two fire engines and a pump truck pulled up in front of the building. The firemen were unwinding the hoses.

Just as Harry came out and handed Mother her book and her box, Walter Sandusky, the fire chief, approached us. "Bea," he said, "you and the kids had better get away from here. We have to keep this area clear. Go next door." Next door was a gas station, owned by Ken Imaldi. He and his mechanic were standing at the plate-glass window, watching the engines. We could see them as we picked our way across the icy stubble of the field that lay between the two buildings.

"How did you know about the fire?" Rosie asked. "Did you smell it?"

Mother shook her head. "No," she said. "Sylvester found it. I sent him up to the attic to look for some New Year's decorations left from last year. It was lucky I did. Who knows how far it would have gotten if I hadn't? It's those damned signs, I'm sure. There's always something wrong with them, and this time I bet the wiring went."

Since Christmas the signs had read "TER IDGE" and "WER BRIDGE N." The electrician had not come yet to fix them. "I've thought about taking those signs down a million times," Mother went on, "but I never did. They're such a landmark, you can see them for miles. So I figured, even if they didn't always say what they're supposed to say, everyone knew what they meant." By this time we were pushing open the gas station door. "You can bet I'll take them down now," she continued bitterly, "landmark or no landmark."

Mr. Imaldi took my mother's hand as we walked in. "Oh, Bea, Min is here, and Luke and Tex. I called my wife. She's bringing coffee."

Mother smiled and patted Mr. Imaldi's arm. "Thank you, thank you, Ken, but I'm sure we'll all be back at work in half an hour. That's what the firemen said."

Mr. Imaldi nodded, though he didn't look too cheerful. "I hope they're right," he said. "But it's a cold night, and the wind is so high." I didn't know what he meant then. I found out soon enough.

We stood at the plate-glass window, watching the firemen. Luke, Tex, and Min watched, too. Part-timers, like Merle, had gone home. "But not me," Min said. "There's no point in going home if we'll be back in the building in a little while."

Dan and I were standing with our noses pressed against the plate glass. "I don't think it's going to be over in any half hour," he muttered. "Look at those flames. Just look at them."

I couldn't help looking at them, any more than a moth can help flying into a candle's light. Long streamers of flame were pouring out of the attic windows, and smoke was beginning to issue now from windows on the second floor. Dan was right. It didn't look like a minor upstairs bonfire that could be contained in half an hour.

The crowded little combination office-waiting room of Imaldi's Esso Station grew very quiet. No one said anything. We all stood staring at the fierce vision before our eyes. The firemen were playing their hoses on the roof. Monster searchlights and the streetlamps that surrounded the Inn's parking lot lit the scene like a show on a stage. The bitter, gale-force winds blew the spray from the hoses away from the building and toward us. Bright, flaming sparks came, too. Sometimes the water froze as it issued from the hoses, and the firemen who'd come first struggled to reopen the nozzles on their frozen equipment while other trucks roared up and new firemen joined the battle.

"The wind," Luke said. "Damn the wind."

"Damn the cold," Dan added.

I couldn't say anything. My voice was frozen in my chest, like those spumes of spray that fell uselessly on the gravel drive, on the parking lot, or on the lawn before they could hit the searing flames.

Suddenly, in a great burst, like the crash of a thousand trumpets, the fire burst through the roof of the Waterbridge Inn. I thought we were in hell.

"Oh, my God," Mother said, and hid her face in her hands. Mr. Imaldi stood on one side of her, and Luke on the other. They put their arms around her and held her up. Mrs. Imaldi came in with the coffee and pressed a cup into my mother's hand.

"They've closed the road," Mrs. Imaldi said. "I had to do some fast talking to get through." She wanted my mother to sit down in a chair, but Mother wouldn't do it. She couldn't move away from the window. None of us could. Dan and Rosie and I stood there, too, like zombies, hypnotized by that fire. It was the most beautiful and terrible thing we had ever seen. In front of our eyes the building died, eaten up by orange flames whipped about by that wicked, wasting wind. More and more fire trucks and firemen arrived, but their hoses froze, too, and the wind blew the spray in every direction except the one that mattered. They were helpless.

Other people came, talking their way through the police lines that blocked the highway. Mr. Neumann, the liquor salesman, arrived, and a few regular customers. Soon Mr. Jensen showed up, putting his arm around my mother, and talking into her ear.

After a while, Min sat down in the one ratty black leather chair in the steaming station office, the one Mrs. Imaldi had tried to get my mother to sit in. She sat with her back to the window. Tom came and she decided to go home with him. But first she came over to the window where we three were standing and kissed me on the cheek. Then she kissed Dan. Finally, she kissed Rosie. Suddenly, at Min's touch, Rosie began to cry. Min put her arms around Rosie and hugged her, and Rosie hugged Min back. "Do you know what happened to Major and Mrs. Dunleigh?" Rosie asked. "Where's Buster?" She must have been worrying about Buster the whole time, but had been afraid to ask.

"I saw the Dunleighs," Tom said. "I went to the used car dealer's on the other side of the highway before I came over here. The Dunleighs and Sylvester and some of the bar customers are over there. Buster is with them."

Rosie heaved a hugh sigh. She turned away from the window and trotted over to the black chair which Min had vacated. She climbed in and was asleep in two minutes.

Min and Tom left. Mrs. Imaldi kept handing out doughnuts. We shoved them into our mouths without thinking, our eyes still glued to the horror in front of us. No one talked much. Through it all, though, the radio played, tuned to station WCTC in New Brunswick and, every half hour when the news came on, they talked about us. "A fire is raging out of control at the Waterbridge Inn on Route 38 in Waterbridge. A high wind and freezing temperatures are hampering firemen in their efforts to save the building, which has been an area landmark for over fifty years. Route 38 has been blocked off from the Waterbridge traffic circle to the township line railroad bridge, and New Year's Eve travelers are advised to seek alternate routes. Chief Walter Sandusky of the Waterbridge Volunteer Fire Company No. 3 says an electrical failure in attic wiring is the probable cause of the blaze, and no foul play is suspected."

I could not believe the radio was talking about us. I couldn't even believe the fire I was watching had anything to do with me. It was as if I were at the movies. It was exciting and I wondered what would happen. Would the fire win? Would the firemen win? But I didn't feel anything. I was frozen solid, like the great icicles that hung from the nozzles of the hoses.

We were watching a terminal case. There was no hope of recovery. I should have understood that when the flames burst through the roof, but it was only gradually, as I watched one piece of the upper story and then another disappear, that the realization was borne in upon me.

Mother realized it, too. Suddenly she turned to Mrs. Imaldi. "Take my children home, please, Ellen," she said. "Take them home and put them to bed. They don't have to watch this any more."

"Neither do you," said Mrs. Imaldi. "You come with me, too."

Mother shook her head. With both arms she hugged her date book close to her breast. In all the time that had passed since we had left the Inn, she hadn't put it down. "No," she said. "I have to stay. I have to see the end."

Rosie, asleep in the chair, could be carried out. But I didn't want to go. "I'm staying with you, Mother," I said. "I want to see it through to the end, too, and I don't want to leave you alone."

"Go," Mother said. "Please go. This building isn't safe either. Sparks are hitting the roof and they'll probably wet it down soon."

"No," Dan protested. "I'm with Rachel. I want to stay here."

"I'll take care of your mother," Mr. Jensen said. "Don't worry about her. We'll get over to the Imaldis' as soon as we can. If you kids go, it'll be three fewer things for her to worry about."

"I'm staying," I said.

"So am I," Dan agreed.

"Rachel can stay," my mother said. "Rachel can help me." She walked over to Mr. Imaldi's desk and picked up a pencil. "We'll make a list of all the numbers we have to call first thing in the morning. The Krauzer wedding next Saturday—maybe I can fix them up at the country club."

"If Rachel can stay, so can I," Dan insisted.

"All right," Mother said. "Stay, stay."

Mr. Jensen was shaking his head, a look almost of awe on his face. "You're a remarkable woman, Bea," he said, " a remarkable woman."

She glanced at him, a question in the lift of her eyebrow.

"You just carry on," he explained. "If it were my place that was on fire, I'd have collapsed long before this."

"No, you wouldn't," Mother assured him. "Most of us are tougher than we think. Anyway," she added drily, "worse has happened to me in my life."

Mr. Imaldi picked Rosie up and carried her out to his car. She stirred a little but didn't really wake up. Mrs. Imaldi walked behind him, carrying Rosie's shoes. He came back into the station while his wife got into the car and drove away. The fire was under control now, and the police were beginning to allow traffic to move on the highway once again.

Mother didn't watch the fire any more. She sat at Mr. Imaldi's desk, turning the pages of her date book. Dan and I still stood at the window, though, staring at the last act, which would prove to be the longest. The flames no longer leaped from the windows of the upper stories. There was nothing left of the upper stories except charred remnants of the frame. But the firemen continued playing their hoses on the building. Bits of fire still lurked in hidden corners, ready to burst up again unless they were found and wiped out.

Now that the drama before us was nearly over, it no longer totally engrossed me. I began to remember things—my books, including *Jane Eyre*; my new black dress that I'd taken out of the closet earlier in the day and laid out on the bed; my four-poster bed itself, and my old desk, and my expensive air-conditioner. They were gone, all gone.

Dan must have been thinking about the same thing. "My pictures," he said. "All those baseball players, all those jazz musicians. It'll take me years to collect them again. If I'll even want to."

"Yeah," I said softly. "I know."

Mr. Jensen's voice interrupted us. "There's no point to this," he said, with a touch of impatience. "Bea, you and the kids can't hang around here until the last spark is extinguished. That could take all night. Get some rest, please. Get some rest or you'll get sick. You're going to need all your strength in the next few weeks."

Mother sighed and stood up. She pulled her coat tighter around her body. I suddenly noticed that it had grown cold in the gas station, very cold. Not only was I frozen inside, I was frozen outside, too.

The door into the little office swung open and Harry Fust came through it. "Mrs. Gold," he cried, "wait 'til you see what we have for you!" He was actually smiling, and his bouncing exuberance was a startling contrast to the icy resignation which had overcome all of us who had been watching from the gas station. "We can't bring it in here," he said. "It's too big. But come into the garage. The boys put it there for the time being. You can decide what to do with it tomorrow."

"The cherry table," Mother said, her eyes lighting up. "Maybe they saved the cherry table." I followed her and Harry through the door that led from the office into the gas station's repair bays. And there, leaning up against a wall, three pleased-looking firemen gazing at it, was the painting. Sir Baldwin MacClough stared down at us, as proud and disdainful as ever, totally unaffected by either flame or smoke.

"I saved him first thing," Harry explained eagerly. He didn't even notice the dazed expression on my mother's face, so satisfied was he with his triumph. "As soon as you left the building, I got four of the fellows to help me take him down. We put him out by the garbage shed and covered him with a couple of tarps. We were so busy until now we didn't have a chance to get over here to tell you we'd saved him. But I wanted you to know as soon as possible. I knew it'd make you feel better."

"Oh, it does, it does," Mother murmured. "It certainly does. Thank you. It was very . . . very thoughtful of you."

Harry's smile grew broader than ever. "I noticed him last time I was at the Inn. The Knights of Columbus breakfast, about a month ago. You remember."

"Yes," Mother said. "I remember."

"I knew when I saw him then that he was really something. I'd never seen a painting so big in my life. I don't know much about art, but I know what I like. I knew we had to save him for you."

Mother was unable to say anything more. She merely nodded.

"Well, tomorrow we'll help you move him," Harry went on, his enthusiasm only slightly moderated by her silence. "You just tell us where you want him."

"I'll have to think about it."

Something more seemed required. "You're very kind," I chimed in. "Thank you very much."

"Well, you're certainly very welcome," Harry said. "Come on, fellows," he called to the others. "Let's get back. We're not done yet."

"Thanks, all of you," I called again, as they left the garage. "We won't forget this." I turned back toward my mother. Her face was hidden in her hands and her shoulders were shaking. "Mother, mother," I begged, "don't cry. It's all right. Really, it'll be all right. Don't cry."

She took her hands away from her face. She hadn't been crying. She'd been laughing. She shook her head. "The painting," she said helplessly. "The painting.

What in heaven's name am I going to do with a thing that size? He was so proud of himself for saving it— the one thing in the whole building that was insured at something like its full value. That's what he picked to save. What about the cherry drop leaf table? What about the Shaker chair? Why didn't he pick on one of them to save? Something I could use. Something I'll have a place for."

"Well, Mother," I remarked, "it's a good thing you didn't say that to him."

"I was hard put not to," she replied.

"What do you mean, the painting was the one thing that was insured at its full value?" I asked her.

"I had a separate policy written on it after that dealer, Stoner, told me it could be worth as much as a thousand dollars," she said.

"And the other stuff?"

She shrugged. "It's all just covered by our general fire insurance. I don't know how much I'll get. Nothing like what it was all worth, you can be sure. There's no way I could have afforded enough insurance to actually replace the building and all that was in it."

I felt my heart sink to the bottom of my stomach. For the first time in the course of that whole long night I really grasped the fact that something drastic had happened, something that could turn my whole life upside down.

We went back into the office. Everyone else was still there, waiting for us. Now, at last, we were ready to leave. We let Mr. Jensen drive us over to the Imaldis'. Then he went back, and with Luke and a couple of state troopers he spent the rest of the night guarding the site. They were afraid that once the fire was completely out, looters might show up.

Mother, Dan, and I dozed on the sofa and chairs in the Imaldis' living room. Rosie had been put to sleep in the only extra bed. In the dark, before we slept, my mother said to me, "It'll be all right, Rachel. It'll be all right, Dan. We'll work something out."

"Yes," I reassured her. "I know."

But the next day, New Year's Day, I wasn't so sure. Neither was she. We drove over to the the Inn to see what was left. A corpse. The ice-encrusted ruin loomed like a skeleton against a cold, bright sky. The attic and the second story, where we had lived, were totally gone, but the first floor and the basement were still there, though everything in them had been damaged beyond salvation by smoke and water. Shod in boots borrowed from the Imaldis, we picked our way through the debris that lay on the floor of the ceilingless lobby. Wherever we went, the odd, charred sour smell of smoke hung inescapably in the air. It was an odor like none other I have ever smelled, and to this day I have but to hear the sound of a fire engine to have it assault my nostrils once again.

In the Holiday Room, the frozen, blackened drapes were pasted against the window frames. The white tablecloths were so stiff they looked as if they were made of painted wood instead of fabric. Bits of burst balloons lay among the soot-coated silver and glassware on the tables. The room was haunted by ghosts —ghosts of all the New Year's party guests who'd never come. It seemed to wait for them yet. The room itself could not understand what had happened. It would wait forever, with its silverware and glasses and salt and pepper shakers and icy, immovable tablecloths and napkins.

I couldn't stand it. I wanted to get out of there as fast as I could. I felt as if I'd run into my own ghost any minute, sitting in a corner, listening to the radio and blowing up balloons.

Mother was in the kitchen, talking to the insurance adjuster. Mr. Jensen was with her, too. The kitchen was more nearly intact than any other spot in the building because it had never had a second story above it, but was a wing attached to the rear of the main building. Ham bones, turkey carcasses and empty beer and soda bottles were scattered on the smoke-blackened worktables. The firemen had eaten when they had had a chance. There had been a kind of New Year's Eve party at the Waterbridge Inn the night before, after all.

"I think I'd like to go now, if you don't mind," I said to my mother.

"But I'm not done . . ." she began, and then she looked at me. "OK," she said. "Let's get out of here. To tell the truth, I've had enough for now myself. Mr. Cordier," she said to the adjuster, "you finish looking around. Mr. Jensen will stay with you. When you're done, he'll bring you over to where we're staying."

So we left, the four of us, and drove back to the Imaldis'. "I feel like someone died," I said.

"I feel like a part of *me* died," Rosie said.

"But the thing to remember," Mother said, wiping her nose, "is that no one did die. Not even Sir Baldwin. It was only a building."

"Are you getting a cold, Mother?" I asked.

"Yes," she replied, with a shudder. "I feel as if I'll never be warm again."

"Maybe it was only a building," Rosie said, "but buildings have souls, too. Like animals."

"Don't be stupid, Rosie," Dan said.

"Nobody was killed. Nobody was even hurt. The worst that happened was that I got a cold." Mother kept saying things like that, over and over again, to comfort us, to comfort herself. After a while, though, she shut up. Maybe even she didn't believe what she was saying.

The things we'd lost didn't really matter. We'd get other things—new books, prettier dresses, older antiques. And of course, ironically, we still had Sir Baldwin. But I felt as if I were floating in blackness. Suddenly there was no center.

X

The Imaldis' house was much too small for all of us. After two nights there, Dan moved in with his friend Gary and I went to Tess Galaini's house. Rosie stayed at the Imaldis' with Mother. Though everyone was kind to us, none of us cared much for those arrangements. It was funny. When we lived at the Inn, we sometimes went to a lot of trouble to avoid each other, which we could usually manage to do in such a big place. But now, living in four different houses, we missed one another. We felt kind of naked.

So after a week or so, Mother found a furnished apartment for us on the second floor of one of the big, old houses on Mill Race Street. The three of us slept in the bedroom, which was large; Mother slept in the front room. We no sooner got back together than we were quarreling again, especially all sleeping in one room. We argued endlessly about what time I had to shut off my reading lamp or Dan his radio, or whose turn it was to do the dishes. But at least we felt a little more normal—though only just a little. We didn't see Min and Luke and Sylvester and Tex and all the various customers and salesmen every day of the week, so we couldn't feel really normal.

Mother was frantically busy. Every day she had long meetings with insurance adjusters, wreckers, people who owed her money, and people she owed money to. She was on the phone for hours with mothers of brides or bowling banquet chairmen, trying to help them make other arrangements. In between all of that, she managed to purchase enough clothes for herself and for us to keep us going. It's amazing what you have to buy after a fire has completely wiped you out—things you never think about, like toothbrushes and boots and a dictionary. Of course, people gave us things, but mostly they didn't fit, and Mother said this was no time for us to go around looking like orphans of the storm. "We're not broke," she assured us. "We had some insurance. I don't want you kids worrying."

On top of everything else, she had to entertain a constant stream of visitors. They came to call on us as if we were in mourning. Most people came just once, but Mr. Jensen came all the time. Some nights when we went to bed, he was still sitting in the living room with Mother, keeping her company as she went through her letters, checked her inventories, read her insurance policies, answered the phone, and examined her date book. One day Dan actually said something to him about it. I was really surprised, because it was not like Dan to ask anyone a personal question. "Mr. Jensen," he said, "what happened to your house in Morristown? Don't you live there any more?"

"The house is fine, Dan," Mr. Jensen said. He got up from the bumpy club chair in which he was sitting and walked over to the sofa, where Dan lounged against the faded chintz slipcover reading *Sport* magazine. "It's a very nice house." He sat down next to Dan. "Would you like to see it? I'd like to show it to you. How about coming to visit me on Saturday?"

"No, thanks," Dan said. He scarcely looked up from his magazine. "I'm busy Saturday."

"I'd like to go," Rosie said, "if Rachel will come, too."

"All right," I agreed. I had a certain degree of curiosity about that house myself.

Mr. Jensen looked relieved. "That's swell," he said. "I'll come pick you up about 11:00, if that's all right with you, Bea."

Mother nodded. "That'll be fine. I'll drive up around dinner time and you can take us all out. It'll be fun to eat in someone else's restaurant for a change."

Mr. Jensen glanced at the unmoving lump seated next to him. "Maybe Dan will change his mind," he said.

The lump had ears. "Don't count on it," it muttered.

"There's only one trouble with my house in Morristown," Mr. Jensen said. "It's empty. It's a great, big house and, except for me, no one lives in it."

Dan put down his magazine. "What happened to your wife? Didn't you used to have one?"

"She left months ago," Mr. Jensen said. "I was sure

you knew that. It hadn't been much of a marriage for a long time."

"Well, I have a good idea for you, Mr. Jensen," Dan said. "Why don't you do what they did in this house? Why don't you turn the second floor into an apartment and rent it out? I'm sure the downstairs all by itself wouldn't be too big for just you."

But Mr. Jensen was not so easily defeated. "Dan," he said, "you have no idea what a big house it is. No idea at all. You'd better come see it." He threw out his parting shot. "It has a swimming pool, and a Ping Pong table in the rec room."

Mr. Jensen wasn't dumb. He said no more about the matter. Leaving Dan to brood on the Ping Pong table and the swimming pool, he pulled a chair next to my mother's desk and joined her in poring over one of the insurance policies she was reading for the seventeenth time to see if the adjusters were offering her as much money as she was entitled to.

If Mother was, at least for the time being, almost as busy as she had been when the Inn was standing, I often felt myself at loose ends. Now that I had all the time in the world to read, with never a checkroom to straighten up, or a bed to make other than the one I slept in, I sometimes grew impatient with my books. I was busy with school work, of course, and with the drama club and the newspaper. I even went to a couple of basketball games with the Crispin twins, where I followed Tess's lead and cheered as loudly as I could, for her sake if for no other reason. But all that yelling and screaming did little to cure the restlessness inside of me.

After one of the games, Carrie, Corrie, and I walked over to Ginty's for a soda. It was the first time I'd stepped foot inside the place since I'd gotten my finger stuck in the Coke bottle. The place was jammed, as usual, with no empty tables, and no empty seats at the counter either.

"Hey, Rache . . . sit here." I moved forward toward the voice. It was Billy Colbert calling to me. He was sitting in an already jam-packed booth, but he pushed himself against Tess, who was sitting next to him, forcing her closer to Carl on her other side. "We can squeeze you in," Billy assured me.

I turned and glanced back at Corrie and Carrie. "It's OK," Carrie said. "We'll sit over here with Janice and Duane. They've got room."

So I sat down next to Billy. He put one arm around Tess's shoulders and the other around mine. He didn't have any other place to put them. "Lucky me," he said, "caught between two gorgeous girls." He gave my upper arm a squeeze. His hand was just as damp and sweaty as it had been that night at Sally's. It struck me as incredible that I could have imagined I had a crush on him at the very same time that I had been listening to Toscanini and discussing Dickens and Norman Mailer with Jeff.

But I smiled at him as pleasantly as I knew how. Billy was here; Jeff was a thousand miles away. There was no point in being anything but pleasant.

A waitress came toward us, a waitress dressed in the black dress and white apron that had always been the standard uniform at the Waterbridge Inn. Ginty's waitresses were not usually decked out in such style. "What can I get you?" she asked, as she stopped at our table.

I looked up into her face. "Min!" I cried. "My God, Min, what're you doing here?"

She shrugged. "I couldn't stay home another minute. All I did all day was cook pasta and eat it. Even Tommy was putting on weight. It may not be the Waterbridge Inn, but it's better than no job at all."

"I miss you, Min," I said. "I miss you every day."

She patted my shoulder. "Honey, you can't miss me any more'n I miss you. I can't wait until the day your mom gets that place back up again."

I shook my head. "I don't know if she will," I said. "She tells us not to worry, she has enough money, but she keeps going over the insurance policies again and again. She knew all along she'd never get out of them what it would cost to rebuild, but I think she's getting even less than she thought she would."

"Yeah," Min said. "That's the way it is with these insurance companies. You're two days late with a premium, and they're screaming cancellation, but when they're supposed to pay *you*, it's another story."

"Hey, waitress," Carl said, "cut the conversation, will you, and get me another Coke."

Min didn't even turn her head in Carl's direction. I did, though. "The waitress," I said icily, "is a friend of mine. I haven't seen her in a couple of weeks and we're catching up, if you don't mind."

Min laughed, that deep, good-natured laugh which shook her whole body. "Don't worry about it, honey," she said. "You want a Coke, too?"

I shook my head. "No, thanks, Min," I said. "I think I'll just get out of here. It's too crowded. I'm getting a headache." I stood up. "I'm going, kids," I said. "I've got work to do. I'll see you tomorrow." Min walked with me toward the door. "Listen," I said. "I'll talk to my mother. I'll find out what's going on. I'll call you."

I got my chance the very next evening. It was my turn to make dinner. Cooking for ourselves had been fun the first few times, but the thrill had worn off pretty quickly. Before we sat down to eat steaks I had over-broiled, Mother took the phone off the hook and put the receiver in the desk drawer so we wouldn't be bothered by the operator trying to get us to hang it back up again. "I want one uninterrupted hour with my children," she said. "It seems that, since the fire, it's been so hectic I haven't had a chance to say two words to you." So for a while we ate our steaks and mashed potatoes and talked about what we were doing at school, and last night's basketball game, and unimportant things like that.

"It's good for you," Mother said. "This kind of life —you know, normal, eating together, school—it's good for you."

"What do you mean, Mother?" I asked.

"I mean," Mother said suddenly, "that Mr. Jensen wants me to marry him."

"I thought so!" Dan exclaimed. "I thought he was up to something like that."

"Is it so terrible?" Mother asked. "He's a wonderful person. You kids need a father. I need a husband."

"Mr. Jensen is all right," I admitted, "but he's not Jewish."

Mother sighed. "If he isn't concerned about that, then neither am I. I'm past that." She looked me directly in the eye. "I can't go on forever alone, you know. We could live in a house. We could be a regular family. We could have a normal life."

"A normal life?" Dan asked, his fair, freckled skin flushed with anger. "What's a normal life? Who wants one anyway?"

"Why, you do, Dan," Mother said. She seemed genuinely amazed by his vehemence. "I always thought you wanted a normal life. I always thought you hated the Inn. I thought you wanted to be just like ordinary people." Her glance took in all of us. "I thought it was what all of you wanted."

"Antimacassars on the arms of the sofa," I murmured.

"Antimacassars?" Mother queried, with lifted eyebrows. "What are you talking about?"

I didn't bother to explain. "Is that why you're thinking of marrying Mr. Jensen?" I asked instead. "For us?"

"If it is," Dan insisted, "forget it. *We* don't need Mr. Jensen."

141

"Maybe you don't," Rosie said, "but I like him."

Mother smiled at her. "Thanks, Rosie," she said. "I like him, too. I certainly am not thinking about marrying him for you. Get that notion out of your heads. If I marry him, it'll be for me. But I think it'll be good for you, too."

"If you don't rebuild the Inn," I wanted to know, "what are you going to do with the insurance money?"

"Look, kids," Mother said, her voice very quiet, very sober, "I can't rebuild the Inn. It was always the kind of business where I just scraped by. I didn't carry anything like enough insurance to replace the building. That would have been too expensive. About all I'll be able to do after I collect the money is pay my bills and put a little bit away for your college educations."

"Couldn't you borrow the money to rebuild?" I asked. "Borrow it from a bank?"

Her face was grim. "Perhaps. But they don't like to lend money to a woman alone, even after all my years in business. So I'd probably have to go to some private lender for the money, at an exorbitant rate of interest. I don't think the Waterbridge Inn did enough business to handle that kind of mortgage. I'd go bankrupt. Or else find myself slaving away day and night. I'm too old to work that hard any more."

"No Luke?" Rosie asked. "No Min? No Tex?"

"Those people are our friends," Mother said. "That won't change."

Rosie shook her head. "We won't see them every day," she said. "It won't be the same. It isn't now."

"Instead," Dan snorted, "we'll see Mr. Jensen!"

"Well, you better get used to him," Mother answered sharply, "because if I decide I want to marry him, believe me, I will!"

"If you must marry him," Dan retorted, "at least rebuild the Inn and let us live there, where I can keep out of his way."

Mother hesitated a moment. "Maybe Mr. Jensen wouldn't like to live at an inn all the time," she said finally. "There's that to consider, too, you know."

"You know what?" Rosie said. "I don't want to be ordinary people. I don't want to be just like everyone else."

Mother sighed. It was an old lady's sigh. "I can't rebuild the Inn," she said. "I can't. I just don't have the money."

"Why don't you sell old Baldy?" Dan asked. "He's just sitting out there in the barn now, gathering dust."

"Yeah," Rosie agreed eagerly.

Mother nodded. "I'll get in touch with Mr. Stoner as soon as I get some of these other matters out of the way. He said the picture might be worth a thousand dollars, and a thousand dollars would be nice. Believe me, I'm not sneering at it. But it wouldn't begin to rebuild the Waterbridge Inn."

"How much would you need for that?" I asked.

"Thirty thousand dollars. Forty thousand. Something like that."

Dan let out a long, low whistle.

"And there's no guarantee we'd get even a thousand for the picture," she went on. "Mr. Stoner said Sir Baldwin could be worth as much as a thousand dollars to the right party. If the right party isn't in the market for an eight-foot painting, and Mr. Stoner has to buy it on speculation, he might hesitate to give me five hundred for it. Of course, even that wouldn't be so bad. It only cost me seventy-five dollars. But don't ever tell anyone *that*," she added hastily.

"You secret's safe with me," Dan said. "Me and my friends don't talk about the price of art much."

"There was an article in the *Times* last week," I said thoughtfully. "Did you see it? An art student bought a little portrait of a woman with a ruff around her neck in a junk store. He gave five dollars for it, and then he showed it to his art teacher. The teacher told him to have it appraised, and it turned out to be a French Renaissance picture worth a thousand dollars. It was a tiny picture, too. Much smaller than Sir Baldwin."

"How nice for the art student," Mother said. "But I don't see what that has to do with us. We know what Sir Baldwin is worth. Mr. Stoner told us. He's an expert."

"Yeah. I guess so," I admitted.

"You, of all people, should certainly be happy, Rachel, if I marry Mr. Jensen and we go to live in a house," Mother continued. "You'll have your own room and no one will ever throw you out of it."

I thought of Jeff. Without the Waterbridge Inn, there would have been no Jeff. But, of course, I hadn't decided whether Jeff had been a good thing in my life or a bad thing.

"But what about you, Mother?" I asked. "What does Mr. Jensen . . . ?"

"Ted," Mother interrupted. "You should call him Ted now."

"All right. Ted. What does Ted expect you to do all day? Clean his house? Go to the beauty parlor? Shop? Play bridge? Listen to soap operas? Maybe you could even join the Civic League."

"Don't worry about me," Mother replied. "I'll always find a way to keep busy. As a matter of fact," she went on, "don't worry about anything. We'll never forget what the Inn has given us. So don't worry. Because we'll work something out. I know we will. We always have."

But would we? At that moment, I didn't know. Was Rosie right? Do buildings have souls? Though a building dies, does its soul live on? Like a phoenix, can it be born again from its own ashes? Or when a thing is over, is it over forever?

XI

In the morning I woke up early. I lay on my back on my side of the double bed I shared with Rosie, staring up at the ceiling. The plaster was cracked and peeling, making the ceiling look like a map of the world, some other world than ours. I made out continents, mountains, seas, and islands. On one of the islands I would live with Jeff, and we would do nothing but read Shakespeare out loud to each other all day and make love to each other all night. I giggled at the delightful absurdity of the thought.

"What are you laughing at?" Dan asked. He slept in a cot by the window.

"Shh . . ." I whispered. "Rosie's still sleeping." I climbed out of the bed and tiptoed quietly over to his side of the room. He was sitting up in bed, a stamp album on his lap, a magnifying glass in his hand. "Where'd you get that stuff?" I asked. Dan had never been a stamp collector.

"Estelle was over yesterday and she and Rosie went exploring," he replied. "You know that little room in back of the kitchen? They found this stuff in there."

"Anything else?"

"Some odds and ends of dishes. A broken down old sofa. A wasp's nest." He brought the magnifying glass up to his eye and peered through it at one of the stamps. "I wonder if any of these are worth anything."

"They belong to Mrs. Akers," I reminded him. Mrs. Akers owned the house and lived downstairs.

"Yeah," he replied. "I know." He turned the page and examined a new set of brightly colored squares of paper. The intentness of his gaze reminded me of something and, in a moment, I remembered what— Mr. Stoner staring through a similar glass at the portrait of Sir Baldwin MacClough.

Dan lay the stamp album and the glass on the night table at the head of his cot. He got out of bed and headed for the bathroom.

"I'm going to borrow this glass for a minute," I said, picking it up from the table.

"Put it back when you're done," he replied. "Rosie gave it to *me*."

I refrained from reminding him again that it wasn't Rosie's to give. He disappeared out the door. I dressed as quickly and as quietly as I could. I picked up the magnifying glass again, found a flashlight in a kitchen drawer, and carried them both downstairs and outside to the old, half-ruined barn where Mrs. Akers let Mother store the portrait of Sir Baldwin MacClough. What a comedown for the Laird of Waterbridge, though I daresay he'd seen the inside of more than one barn in his time.

I pushed open the door to the barn and left it ajar to admit the bright, clear light of the February morning sun. The picture was standing against the wall opposite the door, still covered with the tarps Harry Fust had used to protect it. I picked my way across the barn floor, careful to avoid the rotten boards that might have collapsed under my weight. When I reached the picture, I ignored the dirt and dust that surrounded me, got down on my knees and lifted up the right-hand corner of the tarp. I trained the flashlight on the dark patch of oil paint I had revealed. I fastened the lifted tarp behind the picture so it wouldn't fall back down, and took the magnifying glass out of my pocket. As I examined the corner of the painting, I felt really foolish, like a third-rate imitation of Sherlock Holmes. But I persisted. Flashlight in one hand, magnifying glass in the other, I examined the lower right-hand corner of the painting as carefully as I could. I saw nothing remotely resembling a signature.

I lay down on my belly on the barn floor and wriggled myself close to the canvas. I noticed some thin cracks in the wide, ornate molding that trimmed the heavy gilt frame. All the moving around the picture had undergone since the fire must have put them there. I poked at a piece of the molding between two cracks at the bottom of the painting. It moved. I tugged at it and it came away in my hand. I removed another piece, and another piece, until I had taken almost all of the bottom molding off the frame, revealing yet more painted canvas. This frame was probably not the one in which the picture had originally been hung, and it seemed to have covered quite a bit of the actual painting.

I trained my light and my magnifying glass on the section of the canvas I had just exposed. There was something there. Beneath a hundred and fifty years of dirt, there was something there. I could make out the dim tracing of letters. I moved my face even closer to the canvas, so close I could taste oil and dust. And then I could make out the letters. They were very faint, but I could make them out. R-A-E-B-U-R-N. H. Raeburn.

A marvelous feeling of triumph coursed through me. I didn't know who H. Raeburn was. I had never heard of him. For all I knew, his fame was no greater than that of Stanley Doyle, the Waterbridge High School art teacher. But I had found a signature. In my heart of hearts, I could not help hoping that the signature meant something.

I brushed the dust from my clothes the best I could before I went back into the apartment. I didn't want a lot of questions about where I'd been and what I'd been doing. I'd tell them it was a nice morning and I'd gone for a walk before school. There was no point in saying anything more until I knew more.

The day spent in classrooms seemed endless to me, even more endless than usual. So much time in school is spent learning things no one needs to know. Of course, some of those things are interesting for their own sakes, but most of them are mere busy work designed to keep adolescents off the streets. It wasn't on the streets that I longed to be all day, but in my favorite haunt, the Waterbridge Free Public Library.

The Free Public Library is full of useless information, too, but the librarian doesn't force it down your throat. And you can never tell when useless information will turn into useful information. That is the catch.

I finally got to the library about 3:30 in the afternoon, simply skipping a meeting of the staff of the school newspaper, even though doing so might well jeopardize my chances of being editor-in-chief in my senior year. Miss Newcastle, who had been the Waterbridge librarian since the Stone Age, was ensconced on her customary throne behind the circulation desk. Most people were afraid of Miss Newcastle. She regarded the library as a kind of museum and the books in it as precious treasures which it was her function in life to guard and protect. Every time one circulated, she gritted her teeth. But I liked Miss Newcastle, except when she stood between me and books like *The Naked and the Dead*. She could find the answer to any question. And she liked me, because I regularly made use of that ability.

"Hello, Rachel," she whispered when she saw me. "What can I do for you today?"

"Did you ever hear of an artist named H. Raeburn?" I whispered back. Except for me and Miss Newcastle, the adult room of the library was completely deserted, but no one ever spoke above a whisper in those sacred precincts. From the children's room next door came the muffled sounds of talk and laughter, encouraged by Miss O'Rourke, the children's librarian and the bane of Miss Newcastle's existence. Miss O'Rourke believed books should circulate as much as possible and, if they wore out in a few years, well, then you just bought new ones.

Miss Newcastle winced at a particularly loud guffaw from behind the closed doors as she responded to my query. "No," she whispered back, "I've never heard of H. Raeburn, but that doesn't mean he didn't exist. Let's see what I can find." Her pale blue eyes brightened at the thought of the search, and I trailed behind her as she walked briskly to the reference section. I think she was a little disappointed that she was able to answer my question so easily, for a five-volume history of painting contained two full pages about one Sir Henry Raeburn (1756–1823), plus a photographic reproduction in black and white of one of his works.

I had only to look at that photograph to see its resemblance to Sir Baldwin MacClough. Entitled "Sir John Sinclair," it depicted a uniformed highlander against a mountainous landscape. The face was brilliantly lit, in sharp contrast to the dark background. If the similarity was striking to my untutored eyes, might not Augustus Stoner have noticed it, too?

I read the article about Sir Henry Raeburn as eagerly as if it were a report in the *Daily News* of the latest sex murder. A portrait painter referred to in his own time as "the Scotch Reynolds," Raeburn, according to the article, "produced bold, forceful, life-sized portraits of his distinguished male contemporaries." The article described his paintings as "true character studies," adding that "his fluent, blunt brushwork was ideal for craggy Scotch features. . . . By using forced lighting, Raeburn revealed the faces before him, often almost brutally." He was "a master of the new realism, painting his sitter in his habit as he lived." The article made it seem possible that to someone who knew his work, a Raeburn might well be recognizable if it were signed or not. "He did not found a school," it said, "or inspire imitators."

I picked up the volume and carried it back to Miss Newcastle at the circulation desk. "I have another question, Miss Newcastle," I whispered. She smiled. My first question had been answered too easily. She was anxious for a greater challenge. "How much do you think a portrait by this painter would sell for today?" I asked, pointing to the open page of the art book. "Do you think you could find that out?"

Miss Newcastle turned the book so that she could see it. She scanned the article about Sir Henry Raeburn, and then stared at the portrait of Sir John Sinclair for a few long moments. She picked up the index to *The New York Times* and looked up "Raeburn." But there was no mention of his name. "No work of his was reported sold in the *Times* in the past two years," she said. "I don't keep the *Times* index any further back than that because we have no room to store more than two years' worth of the paper. It's too bulky."

She was silent for a time, a frown of concentration on her face. I was silent, too, not wanting to disturb her train of thought. "Well," she said at last, "I think I'll call the art library at the university. Maybe they can be of some help. You watch the desk for me." She must have really been excited to entrust me with her precious books. She hurried off into the little cubicle where she did her ordering and cataloging, and I took her place behind the circulation desk. She was gone a long time. Three different people came in, selected books, checked them out, and left before she got back. But she was smiling as she came toward me. That meant she had been successful in her quest.

"I spoke to a Professor Seifer," she whispered. "He teaches the history of painting. Fortunately, he was in the library when I called. He said that the value of a Raeburn today would depend on its size and condition." Suddenly she looked right into my eyes. "Why do you want to know?" she asked. "Do you have one?"

My glance fell away from hers. "Maybe," I admitted. "But don't tell anyone."

"Oh, my goodness, I won't," she replied, her whisper now full of awe. "But wait 'till you hear this. A full-size Raeburn, seven or eight feet, in good condition, would sell for anywhere between twenty and thirty thousand dollars!"

"My God!" I murmured. It was all I could think of to say. I stood there for a moment, just shaking my head, and then I picked up my coat and my books. "I've got to get that picture out of that barn," I cried in my full voice. "I've got to do that first thing." Then I turned and ran out of the library.

"What are you talking about?" Miss Newcastle called after me, also out loud, her voice cracking from its unaccustomed volume. But I pretended I didn't hear her and kept on going. I realized in only a moment that I could not possibly remove Sir Baldwin from the barn by myself. Not only was he far too large and heavy, but also, if I did move him, where would I put him? Instead, I went downtown to Kaiser's Hardware Store and bought an enormous padlock. I put it on the Waterbridge Inn account, which, according to Mr. Kaiser, was still in existence, even if the Waterbridge Inn was not. Then I ran back to Mill Race Street and padlocked the barn door. I was not going to be one of those who locks barn doors after the horse is stolen. After that, I felt much easier.

I marched upstairs into our apartment. Mother, as usual, was at her desk, talking on the telephone. Neither Dan nor Rosie was home yet. I sat down in a chair, leaned back and shut my eyes, waiting for her to hang up. When I heard the click of the receiver, I opened my eyes and sat up.

"Mother."

"Yes?" She turned and faced me.

"You'd better call up Mr. Stoner." I kept my voice calm. "You'd better call him right away. It's not safe to leave Sir Baldy in that barn another minute."

"He's all right there," she replied impatiently. "I told you, I'll do something about that picture when I get around to it. Boy, for someone who always hated it so much, you sure are concerned about it."

I smiled. "I don't hate him any more, Mother."

"Well, that's good, anyway." She turned back to her desk. My feelings about the Laird of Waterbridge were not very important, after all.

"Don't you want to know how come?" I asked her.

"All right." Her voice was remote, preoccupied.

I was not discouraged. "He's worth twenty thousand dollars," I said. "Twenty thousand at the very least. Maybe thirty."

My mother whirled around in her seat. "Nonsense," she cried. But she was all attention.

"If you don't believe me, ask Miss Newcastle," I said. "She spoke to an art professor at the university. A Professor Seifer. You can even ask him." I paused for dramatic effect.

"Go on," she said quietly.

"This morning I went into the barn and examined the painting. The molding was cracked and, when I pulled it away, I found a signature. H. Raeburn."

"I've never heard of him," Mother said.

"You've heard of Sir Joshua Reynolds?" I asked, somewhat condescendingly, I must admit.

She nodded.

"Sir Henry Raeburn was known as the Scotch Reynolds. His style is so distinctive that I think Mr. Stoner might have suspected the picture was a Raeburn but, when he didn't find a signature on it, he didn't pursue the matter. After all, he may have figured that the apparent lack of a signature could work to his advantage. If you decided to sell the painting, he could get it from you relatively cheaply, and then authenticate it later, if possible. And if not, well, he could always sell it for more than he paid you for it anyway."

"Just as I was going to sell it to him for a lot more than I'd paid for it."

"Yes, but with one difference," I pointed out. "You hadn't any notion of its true value."

"Maybe he doesn't, either."

"Maybe not," I returned, with a small laugh. "Anyway, what difference does it make now?"

Slowly Mother shook her head. "My Lord," she murmured, "I can't believe it. I just can't believe it."

"Ask Miss Newcastle," I repeated. "Ask Professor Seifer."

"Yes, yes," she replied. "I know. You said that."

"Ask Mr. Stoner," I added. "Tell him he can have the picture—if he gives you what it's worth. Otherwise, you'll sell it to someone else. I suppose any museum in Edinburgh or Glasgow would pay plenty to see it come back home to Scotland. The Scotch are very patriotic." Some dim recolection of poems by Robert Burns was, I suppose, the inspiration for that remark.

Mother rose from her chair and came over to the sofa. She sat down next to me and put her hand in mine. "This is incredible, Rachel, just incredible."

"I know." I felt just as overwhelmed as she did. "We're rich."

"Maybe," she cautioned. "I'll have to have the painting properly appraised before we can be sure of that."

"Well, it is a Raeburn," I said. "I'm convinced it's a Raeburn."

"Rachel." She squeezed my hand. "You really want the Inn back, don't you? You want it back badly."

"What makes you say that?"

"All this business between you and the picture. You used to hate Sir Baldwin so much."

"Well, I guess I do want the Inn back," I admitted finally.

"I can't rebuild the Inn for you," she replied, a small frown drawing her brows together. "It's my life, after all. I can't run your life for you, but you can't run mine for me, either. I have to do what I want to do. I'll have to talk to Ted about it."

"He can't run your life, either," I retorted.

"I don't think he wants to, Rachel," she replied. "He's not that kind of man. I couldn't love that kind of man. But I do love him, and I will marry him."

"And you'll rebuild the Inn."

She laughed and hugged me. "We'll see," she said. "We'll definitely look into it. We'll look into it seriously." Then, suddenly, she jumped up from her seat. "Lord, this is so exciting I can hardly stand it," she cried. "I've got to call Ted and tell him. And then I've got to find an independent appraiser to check out the painting. And then I'll call Stoner." She grinned. "Remember how he tried to romance me? What an operator he is."

Just then Rosie came tearing up the stairs that led from the entryway to our apartment. She was carrying the mail in her hand. "Nothing for me, as usual," she said, as she gave Mother the packet which the postman had tied together with a rubber band. "But there's one for you, Rache," she anounced. She had already removed it from the bundle and she pulled it out of her coat pocket and handed it to me.

I wasn't expecting any mail. I didn't know anyone who lived out of town except Sally, Aunt Faye, and my grandmother. I heard from the last two on my birthday, but it wasn't my birthday. I examined the envelope. There was no return address, but there was a postmark. Toledo, Ohio.

I opened the flap, slowly removed the plain white sheet inside, unfolded it, and glanced down at the signature. "As ever, Jeff Dulac."

Slowly, carefully, experiencing a fearful mixture of joy and sadness, I read the words written out in a neat, firm accountant's hand. "Dear Rachel. I trust this letter will find its way to you even though it's addressed to the Waterbridge Inn, where I know you are no longer living. It is a little late, perhaps, to express the painful shock I felt when I heard about the fire. The news traveled slowly to Toledo. My mother saw a small article about it in the *Times*, clipped it, and didn't get around to sending it to me until a few days ago. I was relieved to read that no one was hurt.

"I will never forget the weeks I spent at the Inn with you and your family, or the kindness and affection which everyone associated with the place extended to me. No one was ever a stranger at the Waterbridge Inn.

"Please extend my deepest sympathies to your wonderful mother, and give my best regards to Rosie and Dan. Know, too, that I will remember you always. As ever, Jeff Dulac."

"Who's it from?" Rosie asked. Her question shook me out of my reverie.

"Jeff Dulac," I said.

Rosie reached for the letter. "Let me read it."

I snatched it away from her outstretched hand. "He

just writes that he was sorry to hear about the fire. He sends his regards. That's all," I said.

"Then let me read it," Rosie insisted.

"Never mind, Rosie," Mother said. "You don't need to read it. It's Rachel's letter."

I folded it and put it in my shirt pocket, safely out of Rosie's sight.

"This is cause for a celebration," Mother said.

"A letter from Jeff?" Rosie's voice was puzzled.

"No, of course not," Mother replied with a laugh. "We may be rich, Rosie, we may be rich," she explained gleefully.

"Rich?" Rosie's voice was more puzzled than ever.

"Thanks to Rachel." Mother opened the door of the cluttered living room closet. On the top shelf she kept some wine and liquor she'd rescued from the Inn's unburnt cellar after the fire. She reached up and pulled out a bottle of champagne. "A celebration," she said. "We'll have champagne with dinner."

"Me, too?" Rosie asked, awed.

"A little," Mother promised.

"Me, too?" I asked, smiling.

Mother looked at me, her eyebrows raised. "You, too," she said at last. "As much you want. As much as you want."

About the Author

BARBARA COHEN, a novelist, newspaper columnist, and former English teacher, grew up in New Jersey in an inn operated by her mother. Today she still lives in the same vicinity with her husband Gene and three daughters, Leah, Sara, and Rebecca.